LORETTA

A CRIME THRILLER WITH PSYCHOLOGICAL SUSPENSE

NADIJA MUJAGIC

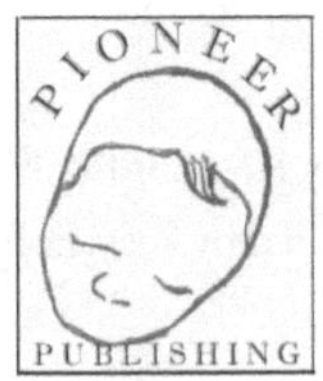

Copyright © 2024 by Nadija Mujagic

All rights reserved.

No part of this book may be reproduced in any form or by any electronic or mechanical means, including information storage and retrieval systems, without written permission from the author, except for the use of brief quotations in a book review.

This is a work of fiction. Names, characters, places, and incidents either are the product of the author's imagination or are used fictitiously, and any resemblance of actual persons, living or dead, businesses, companies, events, or locales is entirely coincidental.

Cover art by RockingBookCovers.com
Edited by Jessica Ryn

A Crime Thriller With Psychological Suspense

LORETTA

NADIJA MUJAGIC

ONLY HOPE and fear propelled her forward as she crawled through the woods, her long nails digging deep into the ground.

It had rained the night before, and the raindrops on the passing leaves tasted delicious. Thirst had made her weak, but the little drops gave her another push. She hadn't tasted water for days. Her clothes were ripped in half, and blood oozed from her arms and legs. The woods were thick, and her eyes tried to zoom in on what was ahead.

Was she close to the finish line?

Escape from the monster behind. That's what mattered. The leaves rustled, and she froze, her heart thumping. She halted her breathing, afraid she could be heard from miles away. If she was discovered, she'd be taken away again. Her head rested on a bunch of dead leaves as she strained her ears for sounds.

It was just the wind rustling through the tree branches, calling for another stormy day.

Finally allowing a long breath to leave her lungs, she squeezed her eyes hard, listening carefully, praying he wasn't after her. If she spent one more second on the ground, she could easily give in and lie there until she got discovered. But the deep stirring of survival inside her had other ideas.

She had to get out of here.

How far was she from civilization? From the first house? She thought she knew these woods well, but the extreme stress had made her forget things. As she kept crawling, she thought she had heard a yelp coming from behind.

Was her monster calling her?

Tears streamed down her cheeks, and she whimpered in desperation. The voice behind her got louder. The rustling of the leaves got closer. Seconds later, she knew her life was about to end.

CHAPTER 1

A Month Earlier

LORETTA'S HOUSEHOLD CHORES, usually done on weekends, were now the highlight of her Tuesday, and despite it being dusk already, she was still going strong. Her tasks included dusting the furniture tops, vacuuming the floors, taking everything out of the fridge, removing the spoiled food, and purging it. She liked her house looking spotless, but the past weekend didn't allow time for house-work, thanks to that strange bug that had glued her to the bed. She'd excused herself from work on Monday and Tuesday, hoping to recover.

The lethal fusion of excessive Red Bull consumption and her disorder-induced manic high was now fueling her. The combination wasn't ideal, but, hey; it got the job done! Her house was two stories high, at least two thousand square feet in size, and not what you'd consider small for a single woman living alone.

Now that she was on a kick, she also polished her collection of more than a hundred dolls, then sorted them by size and appearance in the small bedroom upstairs. The task was a pain in the ass, but she admired her sizable collection, and it was worth her time.

By the time she'd finished tidying up her house, darkness had fallen.

Loretta closed the curtains on the first-floor windows, even though there was zero chance of anyone spotting her. She lived on the periphery of a deep forest, and every waking moment, she faced its trees, lined up perfectly on the horizon. The closest neighbors weren't that close at all, so essentially only intentional visitors could see her from the outside, and those were rare.

Closing the curtains had transformed the atmosphere in the room into something idyllic. She then lit lavender-scented candles and placed them on the dining table where she should have dinner soon.

Her thought of what to eat that evening was disrupted by the knock on the door. She gazed at her phone. It was nine, an unusual time for anyone to swing by. Visitors were rare, and her small group of friends had moved away for better job opportunities, and even when they'd returned for a quick visit, they hadn't gone out of their way to see her.

The knocking on the door sent shivers down Loretta's spine. The doorbell followed the knocking, the loud sound reverberating between the walls.

Should she pretend she wasn't home? Athol was a safe

town, but someone could be there to harm her. Her racing mind couldn't help but think of the worst.

What if the person standing behind the door was there to rob her? Once the question crossed her mind, she grinned. A burglar wouldn't bother knocking.

No, it couldn't be that.

She gingerly walked to the window and drew the curtains just enough to see who was standing on her porch.

A man. He knocked again, then turned around to survey the landscape. She followed his eyes, first looking at the flat field in the near distance, then stretching to the tree line in the far distance.

The man's face looked expressionless. He didn't seem agitated that no one behind that door was coming quickly to open it and greet him. He stood there patiently, as if expecting that someone would eventually open the door.

What could he want at this hour? Almost bedtime. She'd planned a quick snack and a shower before hitting the sack. But his unexpected visit threw a wrench into her routine. Studying his disposition and facial features, she discerned no hint of danger. His patience, a quality she envied, was clear as he occasionally ran his fingers through his hair, his expression unwavering.

Curiosity grew inside of her, and a sudden eagerness to open the door and find out what the visit was all about overcame her. She dropped the curtain and walked hesitantly to the door before inching it open.

The man peeked through the gap in the door and gave her a small wave. "Hi."

"Hi." She looked up and down his body, noticing details about him. Wide shoulders, relatively tall, dark hair, probably in his thirties and close to her age. His jaw was square, and one of his cheeks sported a dimple when he smiled. Handsome. His looks matched his deep voice that projected confidence.

"Hi," she said again, still looking through the door opening.

"I was driving through, and my car suddenly broke down. I wonder if you can lend me a hand?"

Loretta craned her neck to find the offending car that had stranded the man, but she saw nothing. The mature bushes along the fence obstructed her view. The car could be sitting somewhere on the dirt road leading to her farm.

She looked over her shoulder, as if the answer or help lay in the house. She'd never even learned to add the wash fluid to her car. How on earth could she be of help? Loretta had never needed to worry about fixing her car, as someone always did it for her.

"I ... I don't know how to help, unfortunately. I'm not very handy when it comes to fixing cars."

"Oh." The man's face went sullen. They stared in silence until he continued. "Well, I've been driving for the past eight hours and could use some rest."

In a moment of suspense, they both stopped and stared at each other, their eyes filled with anticipation for Loretta's next words. Would she offer him to come in? Would she ignore his plight and expect him to sleep in his broken-down car and wait for dawn to come, then call a local auto mechanic and have his car towed to the shop? Athol was quiet at this time of day; church folks living their unassuming lives, where the crime rate was low, nearly non-existent. But a stranger who claimed to be lost or helpless was a whole other thing.

She gazed down at his hand and noticed blood oozing from it. "Are... are you bleeding?"

The blood droplets fell on the porch, and the man raised his hand, looking at the freshly made wound. "Yeah. I... I fell to the ground and cut myself. I couldn't see anything." He turned around as if to trace his steps.

"Oh, no." Loretta whimpered.

She couldn't let him bleed to death, could she? At the least, she could let him in and offer a first aid kit to patch up his wound.

The man extended his arm toward the house. "Mind if I come in?" He stood there, clutching his hands like a shy kid on the first day of school. "You can trust me. Don't worry." He offered a reassuring smile.

"Okay," Loretta simply said. She had the urge to slam the door at the man's face, but his harmless demeanor suppressed that urge.

Loretta looked him up and down again. Trust hadn't always served her well, but she was willing to take a new turn in her life and give it a chance. Besides, the man looked like he could be Mother Theresa's great-great-grandson. Completely harmless.

As she opened the door fully, she looked down and noticed she was still wearing her flower-print MooMoo dress, which hung just above her knees. It made her look unkempt, especially after cleaning the house for hours. She suppressed the desire to lift her arm and check if she needed a shower by sniffing under her armpit. That would be tasteless, and she didn't want to embarrass herself in front of the man, even if he were a temporary visitor.

Loretta moved out of the way to let him in. She stood by the door, her arms flailing, her hand clutching for the doorknob and sliding off again from the sweat generated by the exchange. The man took slow steps toward the hallway, observing the house as if in awe. He turned around, exhaled and said, "Wow. It's spotless in here."

Loretta smiled. "Thank you."

She was pleased her efforts had been noticed. The man held his bleeding hand in the other, doing his best not to make a mess.

While they stood in close proximity, Loretta's mind reverted to a possibility this stranger might hurt her. He could probably tackle her delicate frame in a heartbeat and twist her body into a pretzel. She glanced toward the kitchen and quickly calculated the distance between herself and the closest knife and planned in her head to run as fast as humanly possible should the man strike. He stood in the same spot, smiling at her, expecting her to say where he should be, what he should do, where he should lay his head down tonight.

Loretta walked to the kitchen and told him to follow her. "Sit here. I'm going to get you the first aid kit."

She stood by the dining table, where the candles still

flickered and oozed their lavender scent. She moved the chair away from the table and pointed at it.

He sat down in the chair obediently, reassuring her he was here to behave in the spirit of gratitude for her generous hospitality. He placed his hands on the tabletop and stared up at her. "Thank you for letting me stay."

She nodded, feeling uncomfortable, and offered him a glass of water.

He nodded. "Sure. Thank you."

Then, after getting him a drink and announcing her need for a shower, she turned around and ascended the stairs to the bathroom.

CHAPTER 2

AFTER LORETTA TOOK a shower and stepped out of the bathroom, she approached the tall, narrow mirror hanging on the wall of her bedroom to take a better look at herself, wondering what she looked like through the eyes of the stranger downstairs. Her body was slim and tall, not an ounce of fat on her. By some measurements, she looked too skinny. But she felt strong. Her body could do wonders, like moving the heavy furniture around, so she could dust behind.

The scar on her lower abdomen was still visible.

It had nearly healed, but she could never escape the sight of it. She ran over the scar a few times with her hand, cocking her head to the side, squinting her eyes, as if admiring it. She took the lotion from the dresser and lathered it all over herself, with some extra on the scar. She closed her eyes for a second while her fingers massaged in a circular motion.

A flashback of that horrible night jolted to her mind,

and she flinched, shaking her head, trying to remove her thoughts. It was so long ago, and she should move on.

Loretta was drying herself for a while, immersed in her thoughts, she almost forgot a guest was sitting in her kitchen.

"Shit."

She ran to the closet to pick an appropriate outfit. The visitor had to be starving and tired. Maybe they should have a quiet dinner together. She could get to know him better, at least enough to survive the night.

He seemed harmless, but she toyed with the idea of placing a knife under her bed in case he wanted to kill her. What was wrong with her? No one was killing anyone tonight! Her manic high phase was giving her all sorts of ideas, and she'd skipped her meds today, so she needed to chill.

After she put on another (clean) dress and combed her hair, she trotted to the kitchen where the man was still seated in the same spot. When she stepped into the dimmed kitchen, he smiled at her.

"Are you hungry?" Loretta said.

"I could eat."

"I made blackened salmon and veggies I can warm up. Will that be okay?"

"That sounds wonderful!" The man beamed.

Loretta went to the fridge she'd cleaned thoroughly earlier on and retrieved a large metal pan with the food inside. It seemed heavy in her grip, but she had no trouble carrying it to the stove. She placed it on the stovetop and turned on the corresponding ring. All the while, she felt the man boring his eyes into her back.

Loretta approached a kitchen cabinet and took plates out. The man watched her intently, as if unsure whether to offer any help, but he stayed put and silent.

Loretta approached the table and started putting the plates down on the table: one, two ... three. The man stitched his eyebrows together in confusion.

"Are you expecting someone else for dinner?"

Loretta stopped in her tracks and raised her eyes from the table to look at him. Her arm hovered in the air for a moment before she placed the third plate down on the opposite side of the man. "No," she simply said.

As Loretta served the food, carefully scooping it from the pan onto the three plates, the clicking of the cutlery against the plates was the only sound in the house. The third plate, untouched, emanated the steam from the salmon, and the man watched it, mesmerized. After a few hungry bites, Loretta placed her spoon next to the plate, wiped her mouth with a paper napkin and turned to the man. "What's your name?"

"My name?" The man looked taken aback by the question at first, but then he proceeded, "Ethan. My name is Ethan."

"Nice to meet you, Ethan. And welcome." She stared at him before she offered, "My name is Loretta."

"Loretta?" he repeated. He placed his spoon next to the plate himself and said, "Nice to meet you, Loretta. You have a beautiful name."

She moved her gaze away from him and blushed. "Thank you."

No one ever told her she had a beautiful name. It was refreshing to hear Ethan say that, because her name was old-fashioned and didn't comply with the name-giving trends of her generation.

She gazed at him. "So, what brought you here? Where were you headed?"

Ethan stared at her for a few good seconds, as if processing her questions. He looked puzzled, as if all that driving had got to him and he had no energy to think. He then snapped out of it and said, "Oh. Yes. I was driving from Ohio to Boston. I have a job interview on Thursday."

Loretta cocked her head to the side and studied Ethan. A job in Boston? That sounded appealing. She rarely ventured to the city, even though, when she was younger, that was her favorite thing to do. She'd walk around the Beantown, check out the Boston Common, walk on the Freedom Trail until she hit Charlestown where the boats on the ocean were bobbing on small waves. "What's the job?" she asked.

Ethan shifted in his seat and took time to think about his answers. Loretta's eyes rolled in exasperation as she grew increasingly annoyed with his slow reply.

"I work in IT. I just got laid off at my job in Ohio and I'd been looking forever until this company called me in for an interview."

Loretta's eyes darted all over Ethan as he stared down

at his plate, now almost empty, and told her about the reasons for his drive.

"How long did it take you to get here?" she asked, curious about his answer.

"Oh, I don't know." He looked to his right with his forehead creased, then looked at back at Loretta. "Eight hours, maybe."

"Eight hours?"

"Yeah. Eight hours. Could have been a little less. I can't remember what time exactly I left my house."

Loretta took the fork and stabbed the piece of carrot sitting lonely on her plate. She cleared her throat angrily as something occurred to her.

By her calculation, driving less than eight hours from Ohio to Athol was impossible. She'd done a trip before, and she knew exactly what it took. An actual trip from Ohio to Massachusetts would take way longer than eight hours. Nine if you drove the speed limit. Ten if you stopped by a gas station to refill the gas tank and a local diner on the way to have a supper.

Things weren't adding up.

But anger stopped her from analyzing further. Her gaze was fixed on the plate as she deliberately avoided making eye contact with him.

"That's nice," she said.

Ethan perked up. "It is. Ohio doesn't have a lot of job opportunities in my field. I've looked and looked and applied, but nothing quite panned out."

Loretta nodded.

He involuntarily reached for the paper napkin on his lap and wiped his mouth. His leg twitched, so he placed his hand on top of it as if to control the movement.

Loretta forced herself to relax. Eight hours could have been achievable if he'd driven a speedy car or didn't have to eat during the trip. She really wanted to believe that if she were to survive the night.

"And you? What do you do?" Ethan asked with a curious glance.

"Me?" Loretta brought her hand to her chest. "I work at a bakery in town."

"Bakery?" Ethan's brows rose. "Are you a baker yourself?"

"Oh ... no. I do whatever they ask me to." She turned to the side and lifted her arm. "I also have a coop of chickens and a cow. They keep me busy."

Ethan laughed. Loretta placed her gaze down in shame, even though there was nothing to be embarrassed about. Having chickens and cows was a norm around here.

"That's cool," he finally said.

Loretta stood up from her chair and reached for his plate. "Are you done?"

"Oh. Yes," he said. "Thank you for the dinner."

The third plate stood untouched; the salmon turned cold. She moved towards the edge of the table and leaned down, mimicking someone sitting there. She gave a mean look and whispered in the air with her jaw clenched, "You didn't even touch it."

In a swift gesture, she made a slapping motion with her hand, as if targeting an invisible head. "Damn you!"

Ethan stared and then looked around the table, as if checking for further invisible guests.

Loretta walked to the sink and put the empty plates inside, then returned to the table to retrieve the third one. All the untouched food was tossed into the garbage can, as Loretta did every single day for every single extra meal she served.

As Ethan helped her tidy the kitchen, his gaze kept wandering to the walls and the shelves. "No photographs or pictures anywhere?" he asked quietly.

Loretta said nothing.

"This is your house, isn't it?" His voice was teasing, joking, but then his gaze got stuck on the round clock on the bare, mustard-colored kitchen walls. Its hands stood motionless, stuck at 8:31. Time had stopped for Loretta, and she knew he wouldn't know how that felt.

"Sorry. None of my business. Lots of people like a more minimalist look. I can change the battery in the clock for you if you'd like?"

Loretta stayed silent, reminding herself he was just a stranger she didn't want to invest her time in. When she was done putting everything away and cleaning the dining table, she declared, "I'm not ready to sleep yet. Do you mind if we play Scrabble before bed?"

CHAPTER 3

ETHAN WALKED behind Loretta to the living room.

Like the rest of the house, it looked spotless. There was a couch on one side of the room, and two chairs opposite, with a coffee table in the middle. On the couch, five pillows were spread at an exact distance, just like the glasses and dishes on the kitchen countertop. He observed the plain décor and smelled the cleaning supplies wafting through the room.

But now he was ready to dive into the exhilarating world of Scrabble. There was nothing sexier than pulling those tiles out of a bag while a hot lady sat across from him, scrutinizing his moves. He smirked to himself. Last thing he wanted to do was play a board game, but he couldn't complain. Though he'd rather chill by listening to music and having a cold beer. At this moment, he really needed a beverage to help cleanse his palate after that awful, blackened salmon. Surely, the recipe hadn't called for the salmon to be charcoal black? If Loretta's Scrabble playing prowess was as good as cooking, he was in for a treat! Not that his cooking skills were any better. But a beer would be nice.

Instead of sitting on the couch or a chair, Ethan sat on the floor, folding his legs under him. He watched Loretta pull the Scrabble board from a bookshelf. The books were carefully organized by color and size. At first, it looked pleasing to the eye, but then a sudden unease washed over Ethan, as he considered all the potential reasons for such meticulousness.

A pang of joy crossed her face as she set up the board on the table. She started babbling about how Scrabble was her favorite game, and that she'd spent a countless number of hours playing it with her father while he was still alive. She always won more often than not, she said, but now that she was an adult, she wondered if her father had let her.

They sat opposite each other, her on the couch, and him on the floor. Ethan studied Loretta's face expression as he looked up at her from his vantage point. He wanted to be sure he didn't anger her. There wasn't a trace of rage on her face, but he could tell her mind was racing a mile a minute. It made him wonder what she was thinking about. Should he ask?

Loretta's beauty was mesmerizing. She exuded feminism with her full lips, the big blue eyes, the dark brown hair that rested on her shoulder. Her slim figure made her graceful as she moved across the space. Ethan couldn't keep his eyes off her.

Loretta looked to be in her own world, ignoring Ethan's intense stare. While she placed the other tile rack in front of her, she gave one to Ethan. She then took the bag full of tiles and shook it, then handed it over to Ethan. "Pick one."

Ethan reached inside the bag. "An A," he said cheerfully.

"I guess you go first," she scoffed and threw the bag at him.

Ethan flinched and retreated. "Okay." He grabbed the bag.

He pulled out seven tiles and placed them on the tile rack, then promptly handed it back to Loretta. A smile formed on his lips when he saw the letters he'd picked. He delighted in the fact that he got a full word out from the get-go, not garbage ones he was usually prone to picking.

Loretta's legs were twitching. She placed the entire hand in the bag and swirled it around and around, counting to seven with her lips, then taking the tiles out. With the twitch not stopping, she placed all her tiles in no particular order on the rack, then bulged her eyes at Ethan, waiting for his first move.

The wind outside made them both pause and look at the window. The wind hallowed and wailed, and gave the house a spooky vibe, building an unnerving tension.

"Wow." Ethan stared at the closed curtains, curious what was happening outside—whether tree branches were falling over, or any damage was being done to the farm.

"Do you think it's going to rain?"

Loretta shrugged her shoulders and answered nonchalantly, "No idea. Can you play already?"

Her voice sounded urgent and stern. Ethan leaned in and chose the letters one by one, as he was placing them on the board.

He first placed L, followed by O, V, E, R. He hesitated whether he should use the letter S immediately or save it for later, but then he thought, what the heck, it was just a game. It might make Loretta smile.

When the board read LOVERS, Ethan watched Loretta's face, hoping it would form into a smile. Her leg stopped twitching. Her wide eyes cast a menacing look on the board; her expression turned dark.

She grabbed her tile rack, all the tiles flying in the air, then she banged it against the coffee table as hard as she could.

"No, no, no, no!" Loretta screamed.

She launched from the couch and stomped toward the kitchen. Ethan heard her footsteps circling the room next door before she returned to the living room, looking enraged.

"Loretta?" he was careful not to sound the way he felt —very concerned for her well-being.

She stopped in the middle of the room and stared at him. Her face contorted into a mask of fury, with brows furrowed and eyes ablaze with intensity. Her nostrils flared as she struggled to contain whatever storm was brewing inside her.

"Shut up!" she screamed from the top of her lungs.

Shit—things couldn't get any worse.

Ethan sat motionless, waiting for the storm to pass. He sat on the floor, slouched, pinching his nose. Having a few beers would be amazing right now. He had the choice to up and leave and come up with a solution, but the storm was getting stormier with each passing minute. His only choice seemed to stay put, whatever might happen with the raging lunatic.

As the wind continued to hollow, Ethan felt Loretta's presence in the room to be just as forceful.

She stomped up to him and snapped, "I'm going to bed."

CHAPTER 4

LORETTA STOMPED up the stairs to her bedroom, then slammed the door. The entire house shook. The lightning followed, making her gesture more dramatic. Not that Loretta cared.

She sat on the edge of her bed, hyperventilating. Her chest heaved with each ragged breath. Tears streamed down her face, blurring her vision as she struggled to make sense of the overwhelming emotions crashing over her. Ethan did nothing to cause all this, yet it was all his fault. She plopped on the bed and spread her arms as if she were about to do snow angels. She closed her eyes and thought about Ethan. Allowing him entry had been a mistake, and she berated herself for it.

She clearly had a lot more work to do before she could trust another person. It wouldn't happen overnight. The traumatic memories didn't simply vanish, and she couldn't instantly return to being happy and normal.

For now, she let her thoughts dwindle as she listened to

the storm outside. She strained her ear for any sounds downstairs, but Ethan seemed to have remained mouse-like. She hadn't even shown him where to sleep or given him any bed linen. Still, the couch would do—he should be grateful not to be sleeping in his car.

She stood from the bed, and, as every night the past several nights, she sat in front of the mirror and pulled a hairbrush from the drawer in front of her. The dresser lamp brightened her face and gave it a mysterious glow. Loretta brushed her hair repeatedly until the pulling hurt. She then moved to the other side of her head and repeated until the other side stung, too. Her hair stood up from the electric charge, so she put the brush down and flattened her hair with her hands.

For a couple of days now, she'd been in the manic phase of her disorder. So much energy. So much elation. She didn't know what to do with it.

Casting a wide smile in the mirror, Loretta imagined herself becoming a famous actress or singer. None of this bakery business that earned her pennies or brought her no fame. Especially considering she had less than five hundred dollars in her checking account right now. It wasn't like she had to pay for rent or mortgage—her father had left the house paid in full—but she still had to make enough to buy food, clothes, and add to her infinite doll collection.

She cocked her head to the side and pictured herself singing or acting on the stage. How wonderful would it be if thousands of eyes stared at her and admired her movements and voice? Her smile widened, picturing it all in her head. She had the looks of an actress or a singer, for sure. Whenever she appeared in public places, she would dazzle strangers and draw attention. The bakery got some repeat customers mainly to see her.

Her thoughts shifted to the stranger, and she smirked. In her mind, the story he was telling her didn't add up. Took him eight hours to drive from Ohio? No jobs in Ohio? Only a fool would believe all that. She strained her ears for any sounds again, but all she heard was the wind hollowing outside.

By the time Loretta went to bed, the wind had picked up even more. It sounded worse than just mere minutes ago. Outside, a tumbling noise sounded, as if objects were moving around, destroying everything in their path. Soon after, a lightning struck somewhere nearby. Loretta flinched and drew the covers closer to her face.

Sleep didn't come to Loretta, even after spending the extra energy on fidgeting, turning to one side then the other, or finding a more comfortable position to fall asleep to. Maybe she should turn the lamp on by her side and read a book, but her mind was racing. There was no way she could concentrate, even though the book she was reading was one of the best she'd read in a while. A murder mystery.

Even though she was eager to delve deeper and read more, she decided against it. Tomorrow, she had to get up early and work at the bakery.

Her mind finally quieted around one in the morning.

The thunderstorm moved away and rumbled somewhere in a distance. The damage to her farm was inevitable, but she'd better think of it later. If she ruminated over it now, there was no chance in hell she'd ever fall asleep.

Her sleep was light; even a slightest noise woke her up. As footsteps approached her bedroom, she froze. The doorknob turned, and shortly after, the door squealed open. A wave of cool air entered the cover as the intruder lifted it. He snuck into her bed and crept closer to her side. She stopped breathing when the body brushed against her. He emanated heat, and she was cold. That was at least pleasant.

Her toes curled at his touch. Her body stiffened like a tall stick. Thanks to all the fuss earlier tonight, she'd forgotten to grab a knife, and that fueled immediate fear. The memory of the earlier commotion surged back, and a wave of panic crashed over her as she realized the absence of any means to defend herself.

Maybe she should scream and tell him to get out of her bed, but she remained frozen in place. His hand moved across her belly until it tightened the grip and moved her closer to him. She held her breath in and squinted her eyes, hoping the stranger in her bed would let her go, stand up, and leave. But Ethan held her close and gently caressed her belly.

That was what she got for letting him in tonight. This may have been her biggest mistake in quite some time.

CHAPTER 5

FLIES WERE MAKING a slight buzzing noise and flying overhead in a circle, occasionally landing on Chief Blake's body.

He was sleeping soundly in his small office, stretched on his chair, feet up on his desk, his arms crossed on his torso. Saliva drooled from his mouth and landed on his uniform. He should patrol around the town, fulfill his civic duties, but the day already proved to be so hot that he had no energy to move. And who could blame him, especially as a man of his age?

It was early morning, and he'd just had breakfast in his office. A bagel with cream cheese and a cup of coffee. The night before, he went overboard and had several shots of whiskey. He'd been drinking far more lately, easing into his early retirement. His agility had deteriorated over the past few years, and the liquor seemed to make it worse.

When he checked out himself in the mirror this morning, his profile sported a protruding, rounded belly. His eyes were droopy, and he looked exhausted. His gray hair was undeniable. At first glance, he could pass for Leslie Nielsen until he revealed his diminished energy.

He'd hoped the bagel and the copious amount of cream cheese would absorb the whiskey sitting in the pit of his stomach. After breakfast, he eventually dozed off, nursing his hangover, fully knowing that the usual quietness around here meant his slumber wouldn't be disturbed. Except by the flies, maybe.

It wasn't like he did this often. Sleep at his desk. For the past forty years he'd worked in law enforcement, and he could count on his two hands how many times an urgent matter arose. Where he lived, a small town in Western Massachusetts, people kept to themselves, and he knew hundreds of people personally, relieved that most of his fellow townsmen were good-natured and decent.

His radio woke him up. On the other side, the voice of his protégé and a young officer, William Russell, informed him he'd located the body of a young woman. "Chief, we've got a situation. Found a body down by the conservation." His voice filled with excitement as if he just discovered another planet.

The chief frowned as the officer filled him in on what he'd seen. Just a mile down the road, another set of flies was buzzing around a dead body, landing on and picking at it, drawn to the blood like a magnet. The body belonged to a young woman, maybe in her late twenties, dressed in a short skirt and a T-shirt and a pair of wedge sandals, appearing as if she had spent at a bar and had too much fun the night before. Maybe she had too much to drink and ended up getting lost and having chosen to spend the night in nature, surrounded by trees. But shit—who would ever do that? It sounded absurd.

And perhaps it could all be true had she not lied on a field surrounded by the woods, close to the main road, with blood surrounding her lifeless body. One of her breasts was cut off and now lying down on the ground next to her right arm. Across her torso was a message from the perpetrator: BITCH, written in childlike handwriting, the letters barely made out. A murder wasn't a common occurrence in Athol, Massachusetts.

"Damn. Any ID on the victim?"

Even with the foul news, Chief Blake was struggling to be fully present and awake.

"Not yet, Chief. We're still processing the scene. But it's not looking good. Multiple stab wounds, signs of struggle."

"Alright, secure the area, gather evidence, and notify forensics. I want a thorough sweep for any leads."

"Yes, Chief. Should I inform the family?"

"Not yet. Let's wait until we have more information."

"Understood, Chief. Anything else?"

"Keep me updated on any developments. We need eyes and ears everywhere."

"Will do, Chief. I'll get right on it."

The radio went silent. Chief Blake propped himself in the chair, trying to process the news. A murder in Athol. It was like getting punched in the chin by a boxer. He tried to recall the last time he'd worked a murder case, but he couldn't think that far. Definitely not with his throbbing hangover making his head as weighty as a solid rock.

He scratched his head and thanked goodness he had Russell by his side. While he seemed a little too excited about these developments, he'd proven to be a good cop and was always so enthusiastic about serving the community. The kid definitely had potential. Chief Blake could see him taking reigns in their small police department once he retired.

No doubt, this murder case would keep them both busy for a while.

Chief Blake stood up from the chair and headed for the door. So much for taking little naps in the morning.

And so much for early retirement.

CHAPTER 6

OFFICER RUSSELL KNEW the precise crime rate of his town as well as the back of his own hand.

He could cite the statistics from the top of his head: last year, there were one hundred sixty-two crimes, which roughly translated to 13.62 per one thousand residents. These crimes included rape, robbery, assault, theft, and burglary.

But none of them were murders.

Zero. And that was something to be relieved about.

Before Officer Russell had gone out for his regular patrol and found the woman's lifeless body, he'd woken up at five in the morning, brewed coffee, and made his chocolate-flavored protein shake first thing before getting in the shower. He'd hummed through his nose as he shaved his beard in front of a steam-free mirror hanging on the shower wall. He was full of energy, as he was every morning before work. Being a police officer was his livelihood and life force. There were so many perks and benefits of his job, he couldn't count them on his two hands and two feet.

Being a minor town celebrity was one of them.

After getting out of the shower, he stood in the front of the medical cabinet mirror and looked to one side then the other, rubbing his stubble. He flexed the muscles of his right arm while holding the muscles with his left hand. God, he was so handsome. He was still single, which he considered a blessing and a curse. A blessing, because he could fully focus on his career and have no distractions, like a wife and children, and all other responsibilities that came with a family life. A curse, because most of the time he felt lonely and wished he could come home to a prepared meal and a casual conversation.

How was your day, honey?

Such a trite question, but he wouldn't mind the opportunity to hear it occasionally. He was approaching mid-thirties, and it would be nice to settle down and have a family.

For now, his career was all he had.

Pleased with his reflection, he smiled, then checked out his broad and hairless chest. He hoped to meet a woman to spend time with, or possibly rekindle his attraction towards past crushes. But things weren't looking too good. The town was small, and the good ones were already taken.

Like Amy.

When he came to the police station, he checked if anything unusual might have happened in town overnight.

The 911 phone log showed there was indeed one call from a man living in East Athol, around one a.m. to report his missing wife. Unease tingled down his spine at the man's whiny voice. He realized then the caller was his buddy, Andy, from high school.

He'd always hated the guy—so confident and pretentious—but now was not the time to air grievances. He'd come across his wife, Amy, a few times, but they didn't know each other well. Amy was missing, and the concern in Andy's voice was undeniable.

According to the call, it was unusual for his wife not to come home. She wasn't really a party girl—never had been—and they had a baby girl at home. Nine months old. Amy worked as a nurse in the Athol hospital, but she didn't have a shift the night before.

The police couldn't do anything, anyway. She wasn't technically missing until forty-eight hours had passed. And it had been less than twelve at that point. There could be many reasons she didn't make it home: did Andy call her friends? Her family? Amy could be sleeping in a spare bedroom in her friend's house after talking all night. Women sometimes needed to escape their mundane lives to feel human again, especially after being a new mother. But Andy said none of those options was possible. Probable, yes. Possible: not in a million years. He knew his wife too well. Amy, a devoted mother, would never leave her baby at home without her, even if her father was there.

While patrolling that morning and heading to his favorite bakery, Officer Russell had noticed something out of place protruding on the ground by the nearby woods. He parked on the road's shoulder and stepped outside his car to find Amy's body. Her eyes stared up at the sky; her skin was yellow, devoid of blood. The muscles of her body had already stiffened, making her look like a discarded mannequin. Her right breast sat next to her right arm. It was surprising an animal didn't snatch it up.

Officer Russell pushed his knuckle against his lips as he surveyed the body. Amy's blood was everywhere, and the scene grossed him out. In the back of his mind, he selfishly thought that solving this murder case could make his career. It could lead to a promotion.

Or even improve his love life.

———

Later that day, Chief Blake and Officer Russell went to speak with Andy. See what he knew. Did Andy have any idea why Amy was targeted? Did she have enemies? Or was this an unfortunate, isolated incident? Anything that could help give them leads to the case.

On their way to the house, Chief Blake asked Officer Russell to fill him in on any other details about the case, still a little rattled from hearing about the murder. They were not accustomed to handling this type of disturbance.

The Chief nodded as he listened. It didn't sound like the husband was a suspect, but he thought they should still pay him a visit home and talk to him. Because, sometimes, when a newborn was introduced into a family, unrest could settle at home, and arguments could ensue. Gosh, he remembered his wife going crazy when he was staying at work until late at night. She'd yell as soon as he stepped foot inside the house, "Where have you been? Melissa was asking for you!" as if he went bowling with his buddies all night.

He'd understood her job as a mother was difficult, but he ensured a steady income. All the tension that grew over the years was probably the reason they were no longer married.

It was possible Andy had lost his cool, struck his wife, murdered her, and discarded her in the woods, then called to report her missing so that it appeared as if he had nothing to do with it. Chief Blake would be able to read him when he saw him in person. That was one superpower he was proud of: reading people.

"What's her home address?" the Chief asked.

"They're on Silver Lake Street."

A forensic crew had been assigned to investigate the body and the murder scene. The Chief would expect a full report as soon as they were done.

When they arrived at Amy's house, a few neighbors came out and stood on their porches, looking eager to learn what was about to transpire.

The chief and the officer knocked on the door and waved at the staring neighbours as a matter of curtesy. But they didn't wave back. When the door didn't open after nearly a minute, Officer Russell made his hand into a fist and banged hard.

Chief Blake gave him a curious look, sensing impatience in the Officer. "You okay?"

"Yes. I'm fine." The Officer nodded and stared at the door, waiting.

The man who opened the door looked disheveled, as if he'd got zero sleep the night before. His eyes were saggy and encased in black circles. He wore a pair of underwear and a tank top, and BO emerged from him. This was not how Officer Russell remembered Andy from high school. His hairline was receding, and his belly had formed into a noticeable pouch. Yikes.

"Are you Andy White?" the Chief said.

"Yes, come in." His voice was unsteady and low. He was swaying by the door like a tree and holding onto the door as if holding himself before he fell over. The waft of alcohol emanated from his body, and Chief Blake turned his head to avoid it. Had he been drinking all night?

"Sit." Andy offered.

They would, gladly, but the place was a complete mess. Baby clothes, bottles, clean diapers, dirty diapers, toys were everywhere, clear evidence of a life of new parents.

"Oh, sorry." Andy approached the couch to clear it.

While he was tidying up the place, Chief Blake looked around the room and noticed photos of the family everywhere. A collage of their wedding photos stood on one wall, while another collage of the couple, with their newborn in tow, stood on the other. Amy was a beautiful girl. Not in a classical sense. But she was attractive enough to turn heads around.

And now she was gone.

Someone at the police station had already called Andy to break the news that his wife was found dead.

The baby's cry broke out in the room next door. Seconds later, a woman came out, holding the baby and rocking her in her hands. The woman looked a mess herself, exhausted and hopeless, as if she understood the gravity of this child's new fate.

Who would explain to the child that her mother was brutally murdered? That she'd had her mother for just nine months of her life, not one memory sticking to her brain?

The woman walked into the living room and handed the baby to Andy gently, ignoring the fact the cops were there. "Can you hold her for a second? I need to warm up her bottle."

Andy took his daughter in his arms, looking unsure whether he was holding her the right way. As soon as he held her close, the baby stopped crying. He smiled, but the smile didn't last.

"Please sit."

Chief Blake hesitated, but he finally did. The Officer sat down immediately, probably feeling comfortable at the familiarity of their past.

"Very sorry for your loss," the Chief said.

The Officer nodded as if to join the condolences. Andy stared at them, not saying a word. The baby in his hands was blowing bubbles and smiling at her father. If she only knew.

"Can you tell us about Amy's whereabouts last night?"

Andy gripped the baby more closely. "She went to go get more formula for Clarissa. We realized we were out, but the store was closing at ten, so she rushed out before it closed." He sniffled and wiped his nose with his thumb. "When she didn't return immediately, I thought maybe she stopped by for a drink at a bar next to the store. She used to do that ... before Clarissa came. I got pissed off, thinking it might be the case. So, I went to bed at eleven. Clarissa was sleeping in her crib."

He paused and watched his baby.

"Then what?" the Chief asked.

"I woke up around one and noticed Amy still hadn't returned. That's when I panicked. It's not like her not to just come back home. I got out of bed and looked for her everywhere in the house, but she wasn't here. I looked outside to check if her car was parked in the front, but it wasn't there. I called her several times, but she wasn't answering her phone."

Andy gasped and paused as if he was reliving the trauma of last night all over again. He shook his head and looked up at the ceiling. Then he lowered his gaze and looked at the Chief. "That's when I called 9-1-1 to report her missing."

The officer nodded, and the chief shifted in his seat. So far, everything seemed to check out. "Then I had several beers. I was worried sick about her. I considered driving around the town to find her, but changed my mind since I was already tipsy." He gazed down in shame. "I called a couple of her friends, but of course, I woke them all up and they had no idea what I was talking about."

He shrugged in defeat.

The woman stormed into the living room, holding the bottle, then approached Andy to take the baby back. When she walked out of the room, Chief Blake said, "Are you two related?"

"Yes. That's my baby." Andy's brows stitched in confusion.

"No, I mean the woman."

"Ah." Andy smiled at his error. "She's my mother."

Although the question of whether he was the father of the child might have been appropriate.

"I see. Does she live nearby?"

"In Holyoke."

Not that far. They'd question her later.

"Can you tell me about anything unusual about Amy's behavior lately? Anything out of ordinary?"

Andy paused, looking deep in thought.

"No, not really."

"Would you say she had any enemies?"

"Enemies?" Andy bulged his eyes at the Chief. He scoffed, "No way. Amy wouldn't kill a fly."

"I see. What about her coworkers? Does she ever complain about her work?"

Andy's gaze glued to the floor. "No. Not really. She

only tells me bits and pieces about her work, but never about anyone in particular."

"Okay. Well, anything else you want to share with us, Andy? Does anything else come to mind why your wife could be targeted?"

He shook his head. His lips went downward, as if he were about to cry. "No."

He hid his face with his hands, and his shoulders shook. A little sob came out.

They sat in silence for a few seconds, then the chief and the officer exchanged looks. They didn't have any further questions for Andy. He was a man in mourning, that was clear. His body language wasn't that of a murderer. That also was clear.

Before they stood up, the Chief stopped mid-air. "May we talk to your mother?"

CHAPTER 7

THAT MORNING, when Loretta peeled her eyes open at six in the morning, the stranger sleeping in her bed was gone.

Outside, the thumping sound of a shovel against the ground penetrated her ears.

Thump.

Thump.

Thump.

There was a pause between each thump, where Loretta imagined the dirt being disposed to the side, turning into a considerable pile. What was going on? She got out of bed and looked through the window. Ethan was digging a hole in the ground. The hole was already a foot deep, two feet wide, ready for a small object to be hidden. Whatever he was doing made Loretta's blood boil. Why was he doing this without her permission?

She snapped her head back and shook her head in disbelief.

Something else took her by surprise. The farm was in an immaculate order. If there was any mess caused by the last night's storm, as the clatter outside suggested, it was now gone. All the objects stood in their place, neat and square, and there was barely any evidence there had been a storm last night at all. Except for scraps and branches from the trees, sitting on a small pile near the hole. Ethan had to have got up earlier than six to clean up all the mess. If this was his way of thanking her for hosting him, he didn't have to.

The sight of Ethan digging made her cringe. Even though its purpose was obvious now, she wanted to investigate. With his speedy and efficient resolve, he looked as if he'd dug holes many times before.

She stormed down the stairs, lifting her dress pajamas so not to fall, then headed straight outside. She marched toward Ethan, her hands clenched by her side, her body stiff as a stick. The heat outside was already stifling, and it was a sign the summer was in full swing. She halted a few feet from him, but Ethan remained completely absorbed in digging a hole, oblivious to her presence.

"Hey!" she yelled out. "Hey, stop that! Stop that now!"

Ethan stood in an upright position, turned around, and waved at her. "Howdy!"

He wiped his sweaty forehead with his arm and gave Loretta a quick smile.

"Whatever you're doing has to stop, got that?"

Ethan gazed at the hole and shrugged. "Okay. I was just trying to help."

"No help! If I didn't ask for it, don't bother."

Loretta was fuming. She stood in her spot a few seconds longer, then turned around and walked inside the house.

She headed to the kitchen to make coffee and breakfast. Her movements were erratic and quick. She almost dropped a mug on the floor. That was the last thing she wanted. She didn't feel like cleaning up the mess after spending hours and hours tidying up the house the days before.

The voice behind her startled her. She jumped and turned around, clutching the edge of the countertop.

"Good morning." Ethan stood at the kitchen door, smiling at her. Did he want a clean slate? "Sorry, I didn't mean to scare you."

Loretta looked at him with suspicion and gave him a slight nod.

"How did you sleep?" Ethan said.

"Okay," she mustered. But it couldn't be farther from the truth. She slept terribly.

"Just okay?" He advanced into the kitchen. "Mind if I sit down?"

Loretta shook her head. "No." She turned around to resume her activity. "I was going to make breakfast before I head out."

"Oh." Ethan sounded delighted. "That sounds great."

"Eggs sound good?"

"Eggs sounds great!"

"They're fresh from the farm chickens."

Ethan smiled and said nothing. He should have some nourishment after digging for almost an hour.

Without looking at him, Loretta asked, "What were you doing digging outside?"

"I was going to bury the scraps. Help you out."

Loretta turned around and looked at him with stitched eyebrows. "No!" she said, then she turned around again and resumed her activity.

The next minutes, Ethan sat in silence while Loretta moved back and forth between the stove and the fridge. Like last night, she placed three plates on the dining table: one for Ethan, one for herself, and one for ... well, one for the person she always left it for.

The smell of eggs wafted through the air, and Ethan's stomach gurgled noisily.

Loretta sat down and stared at the plate in front of her, then took the fork and stabbed the eggs.

After a few minutes, Loretta broke the silence. "What's your plan today?"

Ethan's eyes bulged with surprise. "My plan?" then he seemed to realize what she was asking. "Oh. Oh, yeah. I'm going to find an auto mechanic and, as soon as my car is fixed, I'll be on my way."

"Good," she said and placed the food in her mouth.

Ethan gave a small shake of his head.

After they'd eaten their meal, Loretta again picked up the three plates from the table and angrily disposed of the untouched eggs from the third plate into the trash can. She rinsed out the dishes and placed them on the dishwasher rack before she excused herself.

Upstairs, she put on her work clothes. There wasn't a dress code, per se, but her preference was to dress business casual. A pair of slacks and a blouse. Today promised to be another hot day, but like everything else, she told herself she'd survive the heat. It was the least of her worries. Besides, the bakery had an AC that got cranked to sixty-five degrees, which always gave her goosebumps.

She tied her hair into a ponytail and applied rose lipstick in the bathroom, but went over the edge of her lips, making her resemble a clown. In just an hour, the lipstick would be gone, so she put it in the pocket of her slacks to reapply later.

Once back downstairs, Loretta saw that Ethan was still in the kitchen, poring over the newspaper that had been delivered to the house first thing that morning. He rose from his head when he heard Loretta coming in.

"So long," Loretta said.

Ethan stood up from the chair, looking as if he were intending to say a proper goodbye and thank her, but Loretta stopped him with her right palm up, facing him. "Don't."

Then she headed for the front door and closed it behind her.

The bakery was some two miles from her house. Some days, she chose to drive, but others, she liked to walk when her energy allowed. On a good day, a brisk walk of two miles took about thirty minutes, enough time to allow her to clear her mind before she faced multiple chatty customers, always hungry for a conversation. Loretta didn't mind, but conversations exhausted her sometimes, and she'd come home, retreating on the couch of her living room, and watching reality shows.

On her way to work, she spotted a car on the shoulder of the road leading to her farm. A dark blue Jeep. It didn't seem old, but it sure looked abandoned and ready for a tow. It must have been Ethan's car. On her way home, she'd better not see it sitting there.

Because she really disliked the stranger now.

CHAPTER 8

SWEET THING, the only bakery in Athol, opened at seven a.m. Not 6:59, not 7:01, but on the dot at 7.

Over the years, Liz and Bob learned how to be disciplined when running their own business. It wasn't easy. As a matter of fact, it was fucking hard. Dealing with customers on the daily was one thing. But maintaining the place and keeping it alive was another. There were so many times Liz was going to throw in the towel and declare bankruptcy, because God knew how many times they were in the red at the end of the month. But Bob, being the more optimistic and positive of the two, talked her out of it every time.

Besides, the early forties was too late an age to change careers and start anew. Athol wasn't quite the place they could score a high-paying job. It was easier to think of ways to reinvent the bakery, bring fresh ideas, and lure in new customers.

Bob and Liz were high school sweethearts, married

young, at twenty, and had children right away. It all happened so fast and unexpected that neither Bob nor Liz had time to develop and mature into healthy adults. When infants become the center of your world, your own needs and emotions are easily forgotten. The bakery was their third "baby," but while it grew well at first, it looked malnourished after a few years. The upkeep was too expensive to maintain, and the appeal seemed to have gone. They had their regular customers, but the needed growth was unsustainable. Not even a little TLC here and there.

Bob knew he would look a lot younger without the gray hair and reading glasses. He'd feel a lot better, too, if he still didn't have to pay the mortgage for the house he couldn't afford in the first place. His wife wanted the best and the latest, because anything else would be a shame. Damn this woman!

All Liz wanted was to live a comfortable life. Retire like all normal people. At age sixty-five, if not sooner. Sooner would be even better. She was tired, she was always saying, and could use some lavish lifestyle and have someone else take over the bakery.

As Bob helped Liz to make a start on setting up for the day, he glanced at her face to gauge her mood. She'd gone absolutely nuts when Loretta didn't show up for her shift. Not just on Monday, but yesterday, too. Two days in a row. It was criminal. They only had her behind the counter, and when she couldn't make it, it meant Bob and Liz had to always be there. And how did that make any sense? One of them should be running around the town, delivering goods, doing all the marketing, growing business.

"She better show up today, or we should let her go for good," Liz hissed behind the counter as they were getting ready to open the shop for the day.

Bob stood nearby and gave her a sideways look. "Liz, we can't do that."

"Why not? Tell me one reason!"

Bob stood there, shaking his head, annoyed that he had to explain for the millionth time. "If it wasn't for her father, we wouldn't even have this place."

To start a new business, Bob and Liz didn't qualify for a loan. At least not one big enough to take care of all their needs. They'd paid a visit to Loretta's father, James, a loan officer at the local bank. Her father had approved them a loan of fifty grand—a lot of money back then—but the rest of the money they needed to get their business operational —some thirty thousand—came from his own pocket.

James was an unassuming man, working at a bank 9-5, and spending time with his daughter, Loretta, and tending to his farm animals after work. Word went around the town that he'd lent money to the couple, so he got a reputation of a savior. A man invincible in his own right.

Liz rolled her eyes. Bob knew she was tired of hearing about James. "That was a long time ago, Bob. You gotta let it go."

Besides, James had been six feet under for a decade, mainly forgotten by everyone in the town. His legacy was short-lived. It was time to move on.

"Don't be like this, Liz. If we fired her, the whole town would talk and that will get us to a worse place."

Bob wanted to add that most of their customers came to the bakery because of Loretta, but he thought better of it and kept his mouth shut. That would rattle Liz and bring her to the edge.

"Loretta isn't reliable anymore, especially if she keeps taking sick time and not telling us," Liz continued. "And she's a little eccentric. She's making me nervous. She sometimes behaves like a damn lunatic. What is wrong with that woman?"

"Just because she's eccentric doesn't mean she's stupid. You can talk to her if you have issues. I'm positive that she is more than capable of bringing about change."

Liz shook her head and tutted.

The bakery door opened, and Loretta breezed in. "Good morning."

Speak of the devil.

Loretta appeared calm, as if she hadn't just missed two days of work without notifying her employer. Bob's heart pounded in his chest as he refrained from greeting her, terrified of further angering his wife for being overly friendly towards Loretta. Liz marched to the door and locked it, and Bob stood there, watching her, his face etched in puzzlement. It's past seven, and the establishment was technically open.

Liz turned around to face Loretta. "Where have you been?"

"What do you mean?" Loretta said, wide-eyed.

Bob fidgeted where he stood, uncomfortable about the rising tension. His wife's mean streak could get out of control, and Bob always made sure not to get on her bad side. He walked to the all-gender bathroom in the back and locked himself in until the storm passed. Until Liz got to the bottom of it and told Loretta how it was. And right now, it was grim for Loretta. There were no guarantees she would still have her job by the end of this conversation.

Bob felt like a coward. Despite the difficulty of admitting it, he was afraid of his wife, but he should be there, talking sense into her and moderating their heated conversation. He walked up to the bathroom door and placed his ear against it, hoping to eavesdrop on the conversation, but he only discerned a muffled voice coming from Liz. Loretta appeared to be silent.

Liz just didn't know how to relax and go with the flow. In her defense, the bakery had caused her a lot of stress and shaved a few years off her life. Loretta's failure to show up for work on two consecutive days only made things worse.

He kept listening, his ear glued to the door.

"I'm very sorry," Loretta said.

"Sorry isn't enough."

Bob could picture spittle coming out of Liz's mouth.

"I'll do better. I promise."

"Do this again, and you'll be fired. Do you understand me, Loretta?"

Silence ensued.

CHAPTER 9

BY FIVE IN THE AFTERNOON, Loretta said goodbye to Liz and Bob. Loretta's departure was made noteworthy by Liz's piercing glares. Her exit from the bakery always felt like releasing the air from a balloon after a disastrous party.

As Loretta stepped outside, the heat splashed her immediately. A stark difference from the air-conditioned bakery. She got on the lonely path, skirted along the woods, and put earbuds in to listen to Lana del Rey. For the two-mile stretch, she wouldn't see any business establishments or houses along the way. Listening to music while walking made the time pass more quickly. There was nothing to observe but trees.

And her thoughts. So many thoughts in her head.

This area always looked iffy to her. She had wondered how the bakery survived for so long, sitting on a lonesome land, with no other life in sight. She'd noticed Liz growing more unsettled as time went by, her skin creasing into wrinkles, and her hair turning grayer. But she'd also become more hostile, speaking down to Loretta all the time. If it wasn't for customers who came to see her, she would have quit long ago and found another job.

As she advanced in the direction of her home, her blouse dampened with sweat, sticking to her skin like glue. She couldn't wait to arrive home and take a quick shower.

Halfway, she stopped in her track when she noticed the yellow DO NOT CROSS tape surrounding a block of land. She stopped and looked around, left and right, then she turned around to see if anybody was in proximity to explain what was going on. She approached the tape and stood at its periphery, close enough to notice a red blotch on the ground.

It looked like blood.

In the repressive heat, she could smell it like old iron wafting through the air. There was no question this was a site of murder.

The Bearsden Forest conservation area had a reputation as a hiking haven. Nothing bad ever had happened here. On weekends during the summer, hikers from out of town would flood the area. On weekdays, the retired folks would take walks on the familiar path early morning, then go to their homes—rinse and repeat. There was a small lake sitting in the heart of the conservation, where Loretta had walked many times before. She'd found a secluded spot and sat there to observe frogs jumping around. Occasionally, a hiker would get lost, and the forest ranger would look for them to be rescued.

Murder wasn't common in Athol. The town would surely go crazy with the news.

Loretta quickened her pace, her heart pounding in her chest as she anxiously scanned the surroundings, fearing the imminent return of the police to the crime scene. Every step felt like a gamble, each second ticking by with the threat of discovery looming over her. The desire to break into a sprint clawed at her, but the oppressive heat of the summer sun weighed heavily on her, draining her energy and making every movement a struggle against the sweltering air. Plus, the fancy shoes she was wearing gave her blisters.

As she veered onto the path that led to her secluded farm, a wave of relief flooded through her, momentarily lifting the heavy burden of fear from her shoulders. The comforting sound of gravel under her feet was a familiar reminder of the safety that awaited her at home. Each step forward felt like a step away from danger, a gradual retreat into the sanctuary of her own domain.

She stopped in her tracks when the object sitting on the road caused her to gasp. Ethan's Jeep was still sitting there, which was not what she'd expected when she left her house this morning. Wild thoughts ran through her mind. Had he not gotten the message? And there was something else she noticed now that she looked at the car from a shorter distance.

The license plate was from Massachusetts.

Not Ohio. Ethan was from Ohio, right? Did she not hear him correctly? He said he was driving from Ohio, where he'd lost his job, and drove to Boston, where he'd interview for a job on Friday. Unless her memory was brittle, she suspected the stranger hadn't been fully truthful.

Anger rose inside her. Instead of storming to the house, Loretta trotted along the path, wondering how to best handle the stranger.

When she arrived at the house, the hole he was digging this morning was bigger and deeper. Loretta stood above it, studying its depth and shape. A whole person, an adult, could fit in there easily. It was a sight from a funeral before the body got lowered inside.

The hole led her to so many questions.

She closed her eyes and looked up at the sky, shaking her head. The sun's heat felt good. But the gnawing thoughts of the stranger bothered her. Her eyes darted around house to look for him. Well, he wasn't at the farm next to the house or staring out the windows. He had to be inside, doing—God knew what.

Surprises didn't sit well with Loretta. In her mind, she'd resolved a situation, but when in reality it wasn't resolved, it meant she had to start all over again. Resolving. And it was too much work.

She tiptoed inside the house and stopped in the hallway to listen for sounds. There was nothing. She peaked inside the living room and found it the way she left it this morning. Nothing had been moved. The Scrabble board was still sitting on the table. The tiles that flew in the air last night were spread around the floor. The racks were sitting upside down on the table. Well, that seemed to be a good sign.

But where was Ethan?

Loretta stepped back into the hallway and stood by the stairs. She believed she heard footsteps coming from upstairs, specifically from the guest room above the living room.

The voice behind her startled her.

It was Ethan.

He stood by the kitchen door, holding a knife, its sharp end pointing at the ceiling.

"Oh my God, you scared me." Loretta gasped. She held her hand on her chest, as if protecting herself from an intruder.

"Hi." He gave a small smile that didn't quite reach his eyes. He cocked his head to the side and asked, "How was work?"

Loretta nodded fast. "Good. Good. It was good."

"Oh, great. Well, I was about to make dinner." Ethan looked at the knife, then scoffed. "Oh, silly me. I look like a serial killer." He laughed at his quip.

She opened her mouth to speak, collecting her thoughts. "Ethan."

"Everything alright?" His brows stitched together.

She hated how he pretended he didn't know what was coming. It annoyed the hell out of her. She approached a door in the hallway leading to the basement and said, "Get in."

Ethan stood, paralyzed, watching Loretta intently, as if hoping she would change her mind.

"Get in," Loretta repeated, her voice sterner this time.

He dropped the knife, which clattered against the wood floor with a sharp and resonant clang. The noise echoed through the stillness. Ethan froze.

"In!" Loretta raised her voice.

Ethan rolled his eyes, then, with hesitation, he advanced toward the door and stepped inside the basement.

"Hey, Loretta? Loretta! Don't keep me in here forever, okay?" he chuckled nervously, as he banged the door from the other side. But Loretta ignored him and said nothing in return.

Loretta took the key out of the keyhole and put it on the kitchen table. Bad, bad Ethan. It didn't have to go this way. But what was the alternative?

She'd keep him in the basement until she figured out what to do with him.

CHAPTER 10

CONTROLLING HER SHAKING HANDS, Loretta paced around back and forth, pondering what she'd just done. Was it the right choice? The weight of her actions pressed down on her, suffocating her, as she wrestled with the uncertainty of her chosen path.

She hurried out through the front door without closing it, and let her feet carry her. Outside, the chickens were clucking, but it was almost time for them to sleep, as the horizon hinted incoming darkness.

Loretta had one goal in mind. She rushed through the field and headed toward the place she found most comforting. As she advanced, a bunch of thoughts crossed her mind. The stranger in her house. Who was he? Well, whoever he was, he wasn't compliant with her request. The only way to get sense into him was to punish him. Lock him in the basement. Give him some time to ponder his actions.

Whenever things went to shit, she always found refuge

in visiting the church down the road. She was so charged that it took her less than ten minutes to get there. A lonesome building stood by the woods, a large parking lot next to it, with only a few cars parked. One of them was quite familiar. A red Subaru. It belonged to Father Lee. He lived in a town over, but he was spending time at the church almost every day, attending to services and whatnot.

Father Lee had buried Loretta's father over ten years ago and spoke the last eulogy at the altar. He'd also buried Loretta's mother, but Loretta was a small child when she'd passed, so, of course, there would be no memories or recollections of the event. Or her mother. Loretta still had some pictures of her from when she was young. The last one she took was of her mother holding Loretta and smiling. Several months later, she died, but Loretta couldn't remember the cause of her death. Her father shielded the information from her, convinced it would protect her.

But Loretta thought she knew.

The church had been built in the past century, but its bold structure made it look robust and healthy. A lot of churches no longer maintained the confession process. But hers did, thank goodness. Because if it didn't, who would she talk to? How would she get things off her chest? Who would she tell her deepest and darkest secrets without being judged? Father Lee had listened to her on so many occasions, sometimes asked poignant questions, and would assign a penance for her sins. He'd tell her to proceed with praying Hail Mary ten times. Afterwards, she'd stood by the altar and count prayers on her hands until she was done.

The church was empty. The intricate shadows danced on the pews, while the light projecting between the beams gave the space an eerie feeling. She let out a cough that echoed along the building, fear tingling inside her from the lonesome echo of her own voice. She felt like she was in the middle of a horror movie, being chased by a bad guy about to slaughter her, but she was neither in a movie nor being chased. In fact, as she looked around the church, she knew she was safe. Father Lee kept this place in order.

It was her mind that was a horror.

The church was silent, except for the faint sound of her breath and the steady rhythm of her heart. A sense of peace washed over her, a fleeting respite from the chaos of the world outside. And as she closed her eyes and offered a silent plea for forgiveness, she couldn't help but wonder if, amidst the darkness that surrounded her, there might still be a glimmer of hope yet to be found.

The confessional box was wide open, so she stepped inside and kneeled. She steadied her elbows on a partition and interlaced her fingers while her head was hanging low. It felt good just to be there. On the other side of the box, the door opened and closed, and seconds later, a man cleared his throat. It was Father Lee.

"Bless me, Father, for I have sinned." Her voice was shaky. She wanted to continue and get the sin out, but she couldn't. Silence grew between them, and Father Lee patiently waited for Loretta to speak up.

Nothing.

"May God be with you. Confess your sins."

Father Lee's voice was gentle, like it always was when sinners came forward and sought his council. Loretta was his common visitor, but he always paused after she'd confessed, as if he found her sins a little bizarre and didn't know how to respond. Like, she forgot to give food to chickens. Or she didn't reapply her lipstick when it wore off. Or she brushed her teeth after 10 am that day.

If Father Lee wasn't a serious and honorable man, he'd probably say something like, *What the fuck*, to Loretta's innuendos. She knew he'd never say it out loud, of course. But he was only human: he should allow himself to have swear words come to his head.

As the silence grew longer, Loretta tried to say something. Anything. But seconds turned into minutes, and she still hadn't got the words out.

"Loretta?"

Her breathing grew heavier. Then a tiny sob escaped her. After scrambling to her feet, Loretta swung the door open, and then she was gone.

No prayer in the world would be enough to absolve her.

CHAPTER 11

THE FRONT DOOR was still open when Loretta returned home.

She entered the house, slamming the door, feeling spent from the experience at the church. The sweltering heat from the outside wasn't helping. The silence in the confessional still rang in her ears. Why couldn't she confess? She usually felt comfortable around Father Lee. He never judged her and never would in a million years.

It bothered her. So much.

After she slammed the door, she went upstairs for a quick shower. As she ascended the stairs, she heard the voice coming from behind the basement door. "Loretta! Loretta! Get me out of here!"

Ethan must have heard the front door close. His voice filled the house, tinged with annoyance.

It was too late to reverse her decision. Ethan needed to stay locked in the basement for an indefinite time. It was like killing a person—you can't un-kill them and bring them back to life. What was done was done. But the punishment, as cruel as it was, was the only way to teach him a lesson. He'd rubbed Loretta up the wrong way. There was something undefinable about him she found just so intolerable. It could be his disregard for her feelings or her wishes, or perhaps it was the unsettling feeling she got whenever he looked at her, as if he could see straight through to her soul. Whatever it was, Loretta knew she couldn't continue to tolerate his presence in her life, not after what he had done.

Besides, Ethan's voice didn't sound desperate or needy.

Maybe he was just bored, which was understandable, being in the dingy basement. She found his phone by the kitchen sink, and that was more telling. Who could stand being without their phone for over ten minutes? It looked like he'd missed a few texts and phone calls. So, yeah, Ethan was popular, and not like Loretta, who rarely got texts from friends.

After the shower, her racing mind got her moving all around the house, looking for things to do. She walked to the farm and fed the cow and chickens. She walked around the house, scrutinizing her surroundings and enjoying the peaceful evening settling upon the woods.

Her mind was still racing a mile a minute, and she had to find an activity to calm her down, bring her back to earth. Watching TV was the only thing that could come close to it. *The Bachelor* was on tonight. She turned it on and waited.

As she flipped channels, she caught the local news

reporting the murder of Amy White.

Loretta stood in the middle of the living room, staring at the TV, her eyes bulging at the photograph of the young woman. She certainly recognized her. Amy had come to the bakery more than a few times. Liz and Amy gave the impression of being friends, or at least friendly, as they talked loudly about many things, reminiscent of two chatty chickens.

Liz, of course, complained about everything related to her life. Amy usually talked about her job as a nurse. Loretta remembered her as being softly spoken. Caring. She talked about her baby girl and how she kept her sleepless at night with her stomachaches and other baby troubles.

Loretta couldn't stand listening to her problems.

Right away, she put the dots in her mind together and realized the murder scene she'd walked by earlier had to be related to this murder.

Whatever.

She changed the channel to a more pleasant viewing and found an infomercial selling jewelry. Diamond rings. Loretta gazed at her left hand and imagined one of those sitting on her ring finger. But the way things had gone in her life, chances were quite slim. Her mom's ring was still somewhere in the house, but her father had hidden it in a place Loretta couldn't access. When she was younger, her father would let her try it on, under his supervision, because God forbid if she lost it.

She was in her mid-thirties, and you wouldn't consider

her dating life fruitful. She still dreamed of having a shiny object on her finger and being married, so she wouldn't live alone in this big house anymore. Maybe the community would take her more seriously. Not think of her as a weirdo.

To get herself out of daydreaming, she walked into the kitchen and continued preparing dinner Ethan had started. There was still time to kill until *The Bachelor* came on TV. This time, she served food on two plates, sitting at the table and staring at the opposite side.

She put her knife and fork down and looked at the empty chair. "Why are you not eating?"

No response, of course.

She continued to eat and chew her food slowly while she kept staring at the chair across the table. She rolled her eyes and shook her head in annoyance. "You know, you can humor me at least once and eat the damn food."

No response.

She forcefully put the knife and fork down on the table and slid her chair against the floor, standing up. Making her way to the chair, she slapped an imaginary head and cleared the plate from its path. She grabbed the basement key from the table, unlocked the basement, and dropped the food on the first step for Ethan. She then re-locked the basement door and went to watch TV with the volume so loud that no other sound could ever compete. Including Ethan's voice.

Too bad Ethan was a liar. There could have been a future.

CHAPTER 12

BEING STUCK in the basement wasn't the worst thing that could have happened to Ethan.

Not to mention that he didn't need to worry about his job interview, which, according to his little story, would happen the following day. Or was it two days from now? He couldn't even remember.

He didn't need to worry, because there wasn't any interview to be had.

The only truth about the story he'd told Loretta was that he worked in IT. But not in Ohio. His job was based out of Lowell, a town east from Athol, about an hour car ride on a good day. Ever since the COVID pandemic, he'd worked remotely, sometimes in a local cafe, but most of the time, he chose the comfort of his home. Given his field of work, there really wasn't any reason or need to go into the office. All of his meetings would take place on Zoom or over the phone. Only occasionally, he'd go in when he felt like driving long distance or when his boss summoned him to discuss his annual performance.

He stretched out on the basement sofa, contemplating his next move. He missed his phone, as he'd liked to have at least checked in with a friend. Nobody on earth would suspect that he was locked in here.

He could never admit in a million years that he'd allowed Loretta to lock him up here. And what if she decided to keep him there indefinitely? He pictured his dead body turning into a skeleton, then ashes. Who would ever think to find him here? As these thoughts crossed his mind, he grew more nervous.

He strained his ear to listen for Loretta, but he couldn't hear anything. The house was quiet except for the usual crackles of pipes in the walls.

If he wanted to escape, he couldn't. The windows close to the ceiling were narrow. There was no way he could get through them; maybe only if he lost fifty pounds. The door was too large, and he couldn't force it open with his body. He could smash it with an axe if he found one lying around. But there wasn't anything of that nature in the basement.

He glimpsed at a doll sitting on the vanity, looking at him with its weary eyes, as if wondering what the hell he was doing here. Creepy. The doll was the size of a newborn. You'd be scared shitless if you caught it by surprise in the middle of the night.

Its limbs were plump and slightly chubby, giving it a

cuddly appearance. The doll's face was delicately crafted with smooth, porcelain-like features: round cheeks, a small button nose, and full lips painted with a soft pink hue. Its eyes, made of glass, were wide and innocent, with long eyelashes that seemed to flutter in the slightest breeze. Those eyes stared at him, so he approached it and removed it from the TV stand. A closet in the corner would be a better home for now.

He approached the small vanity in the room's corner and opened the doors. He marveled at the shelves filled with all sorts of food. Chips, cookies, cans of beans, soup, SPAM. On the bottom shelf, there were alcoholic drinks on one side and soda on the other. There was so much food—enough to last at least a couple of weeks. Loretta planned all this well.

He grabbed a bag of chips, feeling hungry suddenly. He gazed at his watch and realized he'd been locked in for a few hours. His dinner upstairs remained uncooked. He was going to make chicken and rice accompanied by a healthy salad, but then Loretta came home and ushered him to the basement. He didn't have a chance to explain what was going on.

The chips crunched as he chewed. Wow, they tasted so good. They'd taste even better if consumed by the TV or on the porch while watching the sunset.

In between crunches, he thought he had heard the door open. He stopped for a second to listen in, then heard the door slam.

"Shit!"

That had to be Loretta. He desperately needed to talk to her.

Maybe she forgot to lock the door. Hopeful, Ethan ascended the stairs, skipping steps. He reached for the doorknob and rattled it.

Locked.

He kicked the door and swore under his breath. "Loretta." Loretta didn't respond. "Loretta, come on! Open the fucking door!"

As his gaze went downward, he noticed a plate of food sitting on the top stair. He grabbed the plate and descended the stairs. The smell of chicken wafted through the moldy basement air, making his stomach growl. He should eat more than just chips, he supposed, to stay strong. Because God knew how long she'd keep him in there this time.

The last few times, she'd kept him in there for a couple of hours.

The last few times, time had flown by because he had his phone on him.

This time, he couldn't believe he'd left his phone upstairs, so he had nothing to spend his time with. This time around, time was dragging, minutes stretching into hours.

But the last few times, Loretta had seemed in a much better mood. Ethan knew her moods were up and down constantly, but lately, she was impossible to please. He obliged every time she'd asked to do role-playing. He'd be a stranger, pretending his car broke down, and she'd be pretending he was a stranger, falling for him. Lately, she'd had pissy fits about trivial things, like the way he loaded the dishwasher or forgot to put the cap back on the tooth-paste tube. She'd downgrade his status from boyfriend to stranger, then start all over again.

The role-playing helped her rekindle her feelings for him and see him in a new light, as she'd once explained. Once they got to know each other all over again, they were back to having a relationship. Until Ethan rattled the cage, that is. And then, role-playing took place all over again.

He was okay with it, mostly. They hadn't been together for too long—a few months, tops—and they were still testing to see where this relationship was going. Even though she was eccentric as hell, that side of her excited Ethan, and boredom was never dominant in their relation-ship. Not to mention her beauty mesmerized him.

He sat down on the couch and sighed, staring at his food. The chicken looked unappetizing, but he tried it, regardless. He stabbed it with a fork. Oh gosh, it tasted like rubber. The seasoning was totally off—too much pepper or something. But he kept chewing it, hoping he'd get used to the taste. After a few bites, he couldn't take it anymore. He put the plate on the coffee table and stared into nothing. As his eyes focused on the floor, he noticed something red peeking from underneath the TV stand along the wall. He jumped off the couch and reached for the red object.

A box.

With intense curiosity, he opened it, partially afraid something vile would greet him. Instead, there were small trinkets, such as a bracelet made of seashells. A ring that looked corroded and browned. There were random buttons and a die. All these items could be of sentimental value for Loretta, so Ethan had better treat them with utmost care.

As he shook the box a little, he spotted a pile of letters underneath, as if intentionally left hidden. Ethan pulled the papers out and quickly counted how many envelopes were there: three.

He shouldn't be snooping around and looking into his girlfriend's stuff. But goddamn, he was so burning with curiosity that he couldn't help it. He only hoped that he'd get to know his new girl better, learn about her past to see if this relationship even stood a chance. Because, truth be told, he knew little about her besides a few basic facts.

He walked back to the couch, looked up at the stairs, hoping, for the first time, Loretta wouldn't bother him, and sat on the couch, opening the first letter. The date on the letter was 2003 and someone had addressed it to Loretta. His heart thumped harder. What else was there to do but read it? The TV on the stand was busted, reducing him to no available activities. Whatever he found out in the letters, he'd keep it a secret.

It wasn't like he had the cleanest record in the world.

He lay his head on the hand rest of the couch and began to read.

CHAPTER 13

Dear Loretta,

I hope this letter finds you well and brings a smile to your face. There's something I've been meaning to tell you, something I've been wanting to share for quite some time now. You see, ever since we first crossed paths in high school, I've found myself drawn to you in a way that's hard to put into words.

From the moment I laid eyes on you, I couldn't help but be captivated by your beauty. There's a radiance about you that sets you apart from everyone else, an aura that seems to light up the room whenever you're near. Your smile, so warm and genuine, has a way of melting away the stresses of the day and bringing joy to those around you.

But it's not just your physical beauty that has me so entranced—it's the way you carry yourself, with confidence and grace, as if you were born to command attention. You have a way of making everyone around you feel seen and valued, and it's no wonder that you're so well-liked by your peers.

In fact, it seems like every girl in high school is secretly envious of you, though they'd never admit it out loud. I heard a girl once say they are so jealous of you, and they all think you'll steal their guy. You know that song, "Jolene" by Dolly Parton? Well, when they sing, they replace Jolene with your name. They see how effortlessly you navigate the complexities of teenage life, how you excel in both academic and extracurriculars with ease. They admire your style, your wit, your intelligence —all the qualities that make you so uniquely you.

But for me, it's not just admiration that I feel— it's something deeper, something that I struggle to put into words. Every time I see you, my heart skips a beat, and I find myself unable to look away. I daydream about what it would be like to spend time with you, to get to know the person behind the confident facade.

I know we move in different circles, and that we may not have had many opportunities to interact outside of passing in the halls. But that hasn't stopped me from imagining what it would be like to get to know you on a more personal level, to discover the quirks and idiosyncrasies that make you who you are.

I understand if this letter comes as a surprise, and if you don't feel the same way, I want you to know that I'll respect your feelings and your boundaries. But I couldn't let another day go by without telling you how I feel, without letting you know that there's someone out there who sees you for the amazing person you are.

Thank you for being the bright spot in my day, even from afar. I hope that one day, we'll have the chance to talk and get to know each other better. Until then, please know that you'll always have a special place in my heart.

Your No. 1 Fan

ETHAN FOLDED the letter and joggled his head. This had to be a letter from her high school crush. As weird as it sounded, he felt jealous, even though these letters had to be written over fifteen years ago. God knew where her number one fan was now.

Where had those fleeting feelings of jealousy come from? They could only mean he liked Loretta enough to ignite the uncomfortable emotions inside him. He used to have high school crushes all the time. But he'd considered himself a cool guy; he never would have gone to the lengths the number 1 fan was doing here. He'd rather burn alive than do something to embarrass himself. Sacrifice was not a possibility during his time as a high school star.

But look at him now. Wasn't being in the basement a sacrifice enough? This woman was driving him crazy. He was getting whipped.

Now he was curious if the second letter would be as amusing as the first one.

Dear Loretta,

I hope this letter finds you in good spirits. I've been thinking about our time together recently, and I find myself unable to shake the feeling that I need to express something to you, something that has been growing inside me with each passing moment.

Spending time with you has been nothing short of magical. From our conversations that seem to flow effortlessly to the way your laughter fills the air with joy, every moment in your presence is a treasure that I hold dear to my heart.

I never imagined that getting to know you on a deeper level would only deepen my admiration and affection for you. But here I am, completely and utterly in love with you, with every fiber of my being.

It's not just your outward beauty that captivates me, though that alone is enough to take my breath away. It's the kindness in your eyes, the warmth in your smile, the way you make me feel like the luckiest person in the world just by being by my side.

I think about you constantly, imagining a future where we're together, where I can wake up every morning to the sight of your face and the sound of your laughter. You've become the center of my world, the one person I can't imagine my life without.

I know that love can be a scary thing, and that putting yourself out there can feel like taking a leap of faith into the unknown. But with you, it feels like the most natural thing in the world, like we were always meant to find each other and fall in love.

I understand if this letter comes as a surprise, and if you need time to process your feelings. But I couldn't keep this to myself any longer—I needed to tell you how I feel, to let you know that you've stolen my heart completely and utterly.

I hope you feel the same way, that you see in me even a fraction of the love and admiration that I feel for you. But even if you don't, I want you to know that I'll always be here for you, cheering you on and supporting you in whatever way I can.

Thank you for being the light in my life, for bringing so much joy and happiness into my world. I can't wait to see where this journey takes us together.

Your No. 1 Fan

. . .

Ethan rolled his eyes and let out a laugh.

"Oh, brother. Give me a fucking break," he whispered.

He folded the letter and put it back in the box. He bit his lower lip as jealousy seeped from his heart. He had to shake it somehow.

Things upstairs were quiet, and right now, he'd love it if Loretta opened the door and let him out. He was running out of things to do, and lying on the couch was getting old.

But there was still one letter left to keep him entertained while being held hostage. This one looked like it'd seen its days, crumpled and torn on the edges. It looked like someone had intentionally attempted to destroy it, but quickly changed their mind.

Ethan sat up straighter from the anticipation.

As he unfolded the crisp paper, his eyes scanned the lines, and a frown creased his brow. His heart quickened its pace as he absorbed the contents, his hands trembling.

The letter was too bizarre.

He couldn't believe what it said about Loretta.

A chill swept over him, raising goosebumps on his skin, as he continued to read. His hands trembled as he clutched the paper, his mind racing with questions that had no answers.

After reading the last letter, all he knew in that

moment was that he had to escape, to flee from this place and the woman who held him in her thrall. The thought of spending another moment in her presence filled him with a sickening sense of unease, a gnawing fear that threatened to consume him whole.

It was imperative for him to get out of the basement soon.

CHAPTER 14

THE MURDER of Amy White didn't need to be in the news for word to spread around quickly.

Everyone knew.

And most people had built their own theory about what might have transpired, who killed Amy, and how ... but no one could understand why. Amy was an exceptionally wonderful person. Not one enemy in her world people could think of.

Chief Blake and Officer Russell tried to solve the murder like two toddlers putting a puzzle together for the very first time. They didn't know where to begin.

As Chief Blake drove, with Officer Russell by his side, to see the medical examiner to find out what he'd discovered, he focused intently on the road and listened to the police radios churning with chatter. Eventually, Chief Blake spoke.

"I called staties for help this morning."

The Officer's eyes bulged as he snapped his head around.

"Yeah? Why?"

The Chief was quiet as he turned to a lonesome and winding road leading to the coroner's office. He squinted his eyes before he spoke, then gave a brief look at the Officer. "It doesn't seem like a simple case to solve. The town doesn't have sufficient resources to tackle the case."

It was true. There were no clues at all. No leads to the murderer. No evidence, nothing. The crew that morning had found absolutely nothing. Not a single hair or a broken nail or any piece of body that would bring the clue who the killer was. And that was frustrating to Chief Blake. They'd even brought the K-9 dogs sniffing around, but it all turned into a fruitless effort.

"So, what's next? Did they already assign someone to the case?" The Officer sounded irritated.

"I'm supposed to find out later today."

The medical examiner was a heavy man in his late fifties, sporting a goatee and glasses, and his head was balding at the top. His name was Arthur, but he preferred everyone call him Art. It reminded him of what he did for a living: he'd previously told the chief he felt examining cadavers was more of an art than a science. He'd been in this "business" for decades and prided himself on the precision and efficiency of his past determination. He had never had a case of the death certificate listing "Undetermined" for cause of death.

"Hey, Art." Chief Blake greeted him. He'd known the man for many years, but he'd spoken to him under different circumstances. Murder was the first time.

"Chief." He raised his brows at the officer.

"Hey, Art," the officer said. "I'm Officer Russell."

"I know who you are," Art said. The chief gazed at both of them, feeling there could be a story behind them, but he didn't want to pry or probe. They had a case to solve. Besides, it was none of his business if these two had a history.

"We're here to find out what you've got."

Amy's body was lying in the post-mortem examination room. Art explained to them that he'd seen dead bodies, but nothing like this. Her right breast missing, a cut from a knife on the right side of her abdomen. The word spelled out across her stomach looked like a nonsensical mess. The remainder of her body was unharmed. The killer had planned carefully what to do with his victim. The knife the perpetrator cut her with was a kitchen knife, most likely just a medium size paring knife extremely sharp if it could cut the skin so deep. Her organs remained intact, too. Nothing suggested she'd fought back. And there was no evidence of sexual trauma. It seemed like she was unconscious when cut. Drugged by nitrous oxide. It still lingered in the body.

Yet none of this made sense, given Amy's friendly nature. Her records were clean. Not even a speeding ticket, for fuck's sakes. So why would anyone kill her?

"All this remains a mystery." Chief Blake widened his

eyes and scratched his cheek. "If it's an isolated incident, it means the killer is just someone random, happened-to-be-there kind of thing. Amy just was in the wrong place at the wrong time."

Art nodded. "It appears so."

All three stood around the dead body and stared at it, saying nothing for a minute. The display was gruesome, but as he stared at Amy, Chief Blake blushed when he felt something stir inside him. It was the feeling he'd hated admitting to himself. He averted his gaze and suppressed his thoughts the best he could and turned to Art.

"Well, thanks for your time. We know where to find you if questions come up."

"Of course," Art said softly.

As far as Art was concerned, his investigation had concluded, and Amy could be buried in peace. Andy, her widowed husband, could collect her body and bid her farewell. Continue to live his life as a single father, lost and lonely.

Solving the case would be a lot more difficult when there was no clue of the intent. Which meant Chief Blake and Officer Russell needed to remain vigilant and look out for other clues. Chief Blake didn't want to say it out loud, but he was happy that a homicide detective from the state department would join the case soon, perhaps bringing the murder to a conclusion sooner than he and Will would. He wanted to end his career on a high note, and now he had to spend all his time solving a murder case.

Not what he had hoped.

When Chief Blake arrived home that day, he felt over-whelmed and annoyed at the same time. Timing of this murder couldn't have been worse. He was looking forward to his retirement and not worrying about whether he'd have to go into work with a hangover. Just about now, he could retire in a small cabin in New Hampshire, enjoy the mountain views and lakes, go skiing in the winter. Sip whiskey after the all-day activities. He was old enough to skip all the mundane tasks in life, such as going to work every day, but young enough to still enjoy life. He could sell his apartment and find a place up north and probably save some money from the sales proceeds.

That evening, his apartment was quiet except for the humming of the refrigerator in the kitchen, beckoning him to search for food. Not that he was hungry, but he should eat something before he went to bed. He walked into the kitchen and stopped in his tracks, thinking. Instead of food, he opted for a glass of whiskey on ice, realizing it wasn't the best choice, given his hangover this morning. But the day was rough, and he couldn't wait to wind down in front of a TV set.

He plopped himself on the couch in front of the TV and slowly sipped his drink. He gazed at the picture of his daughter, Melissa, sitting next to the TV. He barely heard from her anymore. His wife hadn't spoken to him in decades, and it was as if he'd never even existed, never even made a life together in the form of their beautiful daughter. He was profoundly sad but didn't dwell on it too much.

Hours and hours of mediating taught him to live in the present.

Whiskey got him drunk easily, so he'd better be careful about how much he had. He turned the TV on and cruised through the channels, but nothing of interest stuck. His eyes rolled in his sockets when a rush of desire coursed through him. Amy's dead body crossed his mind, and he hated how it turned him on. He was sick. Absolutely goddamn sick.

Was it called necrophilia?

In his defense, he'd never have sex with a dead body. He would never go that far. He'd just stare at them infinitely and jerk off to the image. Like he'd done many times before.

That was probably the reason his wife left him. He was sick. She'd caught him once sitting at his desk, naked, staring at the photos of dead bodies he'd found in the police database. She divorced him immediately, realizing her perfect marriage was a lie. It wasn't because he worked hard and showed up at home in a wee hour skipping all the help at home she needed from him. Only a selfish asshole would divorce a husband for working hard. And his wife was one of the most giving women. But she didn't do it for him. Every time they had intercourse, he'd picture her dead. She was too alive and moving too much for him to enjoy her. It was a way for him to detach. To protect himself from getting hurt.

He put his whiskey glass down on the coffee table and

unzipped his pants. He was as hard as a rock, so he rubbed himself, thinking of Amy. Goddamn sick mind. But he ignored it for now. A few minutes later, he yelped in pleasure as he orgasmed, forgetting how sick he really was.

CHAPTER 15

THE FOLLOWING DAY WAS COOLER, so Loretta walked to work, finding a perfect way to think about what to do with Ethan.

She had to let him out at some point. Not until she'd decided where this relationship was going, though. Loretta had always faced major problems in her life because of her diagnosis with bi-polar when she was a teenager. From mood swings—high energy to deep depression—to feeling isolated and unable to connect with others, to engaging in all sorts of destructive behaviors, she had it all. And wasn't proud of it.

But don't even get her started on having a meaningful relationship. Ethan was the first person who seemed to tolerate her "disease." She questioned how long they'd last, and her guess was not long, because he was making her angry all the time. She'd spelled out all the rules to him when they dated, and he still ignored them. Dipshit. She hated his arrogance, and he'd need to pay for it.

She must be doing something wrong, though. Plenty of people had bipolar and would never dream of doing some of the things that she's done. But she wouldn't think about that right now.

Lately, she'd skipped taking her medication because she was sick and tired of being tied to it. It was a daily chore she'd never gotten used to. And never would. As for Ethan, there was no way in hell this relationship would last. None of them did.

Goodness, how much she'd wanted that. She was approaching mid-thirties, and she dreamed of being in a healthy relationship with a man who would understand all the nuances of her personality. Wouldn't it be awesome to have someone to love unconditionally? Whatever that meant. Her father used to say there was no such a thing as loving unconditionally in adulthood. Everyone expects something in return, whether they admit it or not.

Fine. That was fine with Loretta. She would give to the right person. Part of her felt that being tied to someone had its privileges. No more strange looks at the weird single woman.

Rage coursed through her veins as she thought about all the people who'd wronged her over the years. Just how many times did she want to harm herself and end her life to avoid all the shame?

Someone should pay for it.

Her thoughts upset her so much that she didn't realize she'd hastened her steps, oblivious to her surroundings. She'd passed the murder scene without taking notice. She showed up at the bakery a few minutes before seven. Dressed in her usual work "uniform" and the lipstick on, she was ready to work.

Liz huffed and puffed at the sight of Loretta walking through the door. Bob just gave her a nod from behind his computer in the back corner.

Loretta made no eye contact as she found things to do around the bakery.

Ten minutes past seven, their first customer arrived. It was Officer Russell. He looked dashing as always and sexy in his uniform. The smell of cologne overrode the smell of bread as soon as he stepped inside the bakery. He must have been getting ready to tackle his day as soon as he'd had his favorite donut with strawberry jelly inside.

He strode to the counter and gazed at the menu board above, then checked the pastries displayed in the case. "Morning."

Bob raised his head from the computer and said, "Hey, officer, how are you doing?"

He turned to face Bob. "Not bad. And yourself?"

Bob took his reading eyeglasses off and held them in the air, "Well, things are okay, I guess." He paused. "Any news on the murder victim?"

The officer squinted at Bob, making him squirm. "No. Nothing yet."

Bob nodded, and Loretta realized what was behind the worry in his eyes. Now that the town was shaken, their livelihood could depend on the killer being caught.

When people got scared, they did extraordinary things. And sometimes, they'd hide at home to avoid getting murdered.

Liz interjected as she came from around the corner. "Any leads?"

She caught him staring at Loretta as she arranged pastries on the shelves. The annoyance in her voice grew as she repeated her question, a little louder this time. "Any leads, officer?"

He turned to her and said, "No. No leads yet."

"It's so bizarre that someone would kill Amy. She used to come here all the time to get bread. But when she had a baby, we didn't see her much at all." Liz sniffled and made a sad face.

The officer nodded, then his eyes met with Loretta's for a moment. "Hey, Loretta."

His voice sounded soft.

Loretta gave a quick nod and averted her gaze. She preferred to stay in her lane, do her work, and go home when the time came.

"Hey," she said, without looking at him.

She felt her cheeks redden at the mention of her name. Liz scoffed and carried on a conversation with the officer.

She pulled a scone out of the case and put it in a paper bag with the jelly donut. Extending her arm, she said, "This is from me. For later."

Then she said, "Keep us posted on the case, will you?"

He nodded and ran his hand over his hair. "Sure." He hesitated for a second, then said, "We're getting help from the state police. I'm meeting with the newly assigned homicide detective tomorrow."

He glanced at Loretta, then at Liz and shrugged. "Something about our department not having enough resources." He chuckled.

"I guess that's a good thing, right?" Liz said.

"Yeah." He bit down on his lower lip. The envy in his voice was obvious. "Yeah."

———

By the time the bakery closed, Liz felt exhausted.

And it wasn't physical exhaustion that bothered her. There was something more malicious and sinister that took all her energy away, but she couldn't quite put her finger on it. It had to be accumulated stress. She couldn't wait to get home and relax. She pictured herself sitting on the sofa in her living room with a glass of red wine. She'd call her children and talk to them, see how they were doing. Maybe even plan a vacation soon, with all of them together. She and Bob couldn't really afford to close the bakery for a week, but what the hell? Life was too short, plus they'd done nothing like it while they were adults.

Bob had already left, and she was set to close the business for the day. As always, she'd count the money, close the register, and take the trash out. The routine was so engrained in her brain that she could do it in her sleep. As she opened the cubby in the kitchen to take the trash out, something caught her eye. She stopped from pulling the trash bag and released it from her hands. Her eyes squinted, zeroing in on the object sitting on the floor, but she still couldn't discern what it was. She bent down further and kneeled on the floor for better access. The trash can was in the way, so she moved it to the side.

She gasped.

The bloody knife was at a full display.

Her eyes bulged, and she placed her hand on her mouth in utter shock. "Oh, my God," she whispered. It was her worst nightmare. Her heart was hammering in her chest, and she had a hard time breathing.

How did this get here?

This was undeniable proof of a homicide. This had to be the knife that killed Amy. What else could it be? Sure, the bakery supplied all kinds of knives, but this was not it, even though it looked like it could have come straight from the kitchen. She wanted to grab the knife and put it somewhere safe, but she thought better of it. Best not to touch it. The best thing she could do was call the cops and let them deal with it. She stood up and reached for her phone, dialing Officer Russell. The phone rang a few times, then went into voicemail. Maybe this wasn't such a good idea. Calling a cop on his personal phone.

Her hands were shaking as she dialed 9-1-1. She flexed her jaw as if to warm it up before she spoke to the dispatcher to report the bloody knife.

The dispatcher took the information, and when she hung up, her phone rang. It was Will—Officer Russell.

"Hey, Liz. What's up?" He sounded upbeat, like he was just working out or something.

"I just found a bloody knife in the trash. Will, I'm scared." She filled him in on the details, and her own personal theory as to how it got there.

Silence. "Listen, Liz. I'll be right there. Lock the bakery and stay put, okay?"

She nodded, not saying a word. Relief engulfed her as she realized the personal connection she had with him was a great perk.

CHAPTER 16

"CHIEF, WE GOT A CALL." The Officer stormed into his office without knocking. It was eight o'clock in the evening, and they were both still in the office. Nothing better to do.

The Chief put his phone down. "What kind of call?"

"We might have our first suspect in the case."

The Chief creased his eyebrows, somewhat surprised. The murder scene had provided no evidence or leads. A flicker of relief fluttered through him. At least something was finally happening. They'd have at least something to present once the detective got assigned and they briefed him, even if it came to nothing in the end.

Chief Blake leaned forward at his desk. "I'm listening."

"The owner of the bakery on the east side of town, *Sweet Thing,* her name is Liz, called a few minutes ago to report finding a bloody knife under the trash can in the bakery kitchen. She believes one of her employees, Loretta, hid it there."

The Chief lifted his eyebrows and said, "Okay."

He expected him to go on.

"The murder took place close to the bakery, so Liz just assumed that it had to be her, because no one else has access to the kitchen."

"No one? What about bakers? Liz does all the baking?"

The officer shook his head. "Well, she has a baker, but she's been out the last few days with the flu. She even has a doctor's note."

"I see." Chief Blake leaned against the chair and swirled it around. He tapped the desktop with his fingers and said, "Who else has access to the kitchen besides Loretta and Liz?"

The officer paused for a second and fired, "Liz's husband Bob."

"So, it couldn't be him who left the bloody knife?" The Chief hated plot holes in an investigation. The officer was young, and he still had a lot of learning to do. But darn it, he couldn't just take it all for granted, based on what the woman said.

"I've known Bob for years, and he's a good guy. I've already checked his records, and he's clean as a whistle." He waited for the Chief to respond, but he said nothing. "Anyway, she'll be in the bakery until we arrive and collect the evidence."

The Chief stood up from his chair with difficulty. "Let's go."

The problem was he'd had too much whiskey the previous night, and the next day's hangover slowed him down. He hated when that happened, and it was getting worse and worse as he aged. But when he retired, he would not have to worry about hangovers or the next days. He could sleep in every day, stay in bed all day, and fill his days as he pleased. He couldn't wait.

On their way to the bakery, the officer drove with the chief by his side. Chief Blake had visited this bakery several times, but it was out of the way to his house, so it was only when he was patrolling around the town. Besides, it wasn't like he could eat pastries whenever he wanted. He wasn't Officer Russell, in his thirties, losing weight at a whim or building muscle like it was Lego.

They arrived at the bakery, carefully tapping on the front door. Liz seemed to struggle with opening the door, and her hands were shaking. When the chief and the officer entered the premises, she bore her eyes into the officer's as if she was pleading for help. She lifted her arm and pointed at the back of the room. "There."

The kitchen space at the back was half-dim and eerily silent, like the set of a horror movie.

The two men walked in and found the bloody knife. The Chief took photographs, put gloves on and collected it for forensic analysis later on, hoping to confirm it was related to Amy's murder or that any fingerprints would identify the suspect, or discover more circumstantial evidence.

But who would be stupid enough to leave the knife in a bakery trash can? Whoever did it didn't think things through, that was for sure.

When they collected the evidence, Chief Blake went

to speak with Liz. He found her sitting in a chair at one of the circle tables out front, staring at her phone. Her eyes were red and puffy.

"Does the bakery have surveillance cameras?"

She lifted her head to meet the Chief's eyes and shook her head. "No. No cameras." She cocked her head to the side and made a sad face. "We can't really afford them."

The chief shook his head. "Alright."

Chief Blake looked around, noticing the broken tile on the floor, and the wood on the counter chipped on the side. The overhead menu had a few letters missing, and now that he had time to observe and reflect, he realized this place was a shithole.

An involuntary cough caught him by surprise. "Where is your husband now?"

"My husband? He's probably at home, making dinner." She took her phone and her eyes widened when she looked down at her screen. "Looks like he's called me several times. He's probably wondering where I am."

"Okay," Chief Blake said. "What is your address, ma'am?"

"My address?" Liz's eyes bulged at the chief. She gave their home address with a trembling voice.

The chief looked at the officer and nodded. "Let's first go talk to Bob."

"Yes, Chief."

He turned to Liz. "If you see anything unusual, call us immediately."

"Will do."

———

Talking to Bob led to nothing. He had a perfect alibi.

Not only did he genuinely look concerned about his wife finding the murder evidence, but he also offered to do whatever was in his power to advance the investigation—look out for clues, talk to customers, see if anyone would shed light on the case.

The chief and the officer crossed him off their suspect list.

At the police station, the chief had delivered the evidence piece to the forensic lab. While they waited for the results, he checked in with the officer to see if anything surfaced about their prime suspect. Earlier, he said he'd look for more information about Loretta. Hopefully, there would be enough to tie her to the murder case.

Chief Blake hung out in the office, feeling a little bleak and numb. He should be happy that they had something to work with, but he felt depleted. He wasn't sure if the hangover was still in effect, or what, but he just cared little about what was going to happen to the case. In all honesty, he'd rather Officer Russell do the groundwork. He would just supervise. The next day, the homicide detective would join them. Things would get easier. One could only hope.

As if his wishes had been heard, the officer entered his office an hour later with some news.

"Hey, Chief. I investigated our suspect. Checked her criminal records. She's clean, but she does have several speeding tickets in the past year."

The chief raised his eyebrows. "How many?"

"Four, just in the past year," the officer said. "Her driver's license was suspended for a month after getting three tickets, but then she got another speeding ticket after it got reinstated. She has been locked up in a psych ward several times after disturbing peace and allegedly attempting suicide. Apparently diagnosed with bi-polar."

None of this suggested she could be the murderer, but it was worth questioning her. According to the chief, someone who was willing to harm themselves could equally harm others. So, it wasn't so far-fetched.

"Where does she live?" the chief probed.

"On the other side of town. As a matter of fact, not that far from the bakery." He paused, then added, "The murder took place between the bakery and her house."

Well, shit. Things were getting more interesting by the minute.

The chief rose from his chair and said, "You have her address, right?"

"Yes, sir."

"Let's go."

They exited the police building just as the darkness enveloped the town.

CHAPTER 17

THE BACHELOR WAS on the TV at full blast.

Loretta was sitting on her couch in the living room, eating popcorn and soaking in every little detail of the reality show. It was one of the last episodes, with only three girls left for the bachelor to choose from. She fixated her eyes on the screen, scrutinizing every little move by the girls, the way they dressed and spoke, flirting their way into the guy's life. She was wondering which one he'd pick. If she were ever on the show, she wondered how she'd be with so many women around. The competition was fierce.

She picked up her phone and thought of someone to share her thoughts with, but no one came to mind. Not a soul to talk to. Letting Ethan out of the basement and watching TV with him while commenting on the show crossed her mind. But she was afraid to let him out. She pictured him like a wild animal getting out of the cage, enraged that his freedom had been taken away for trivial reasons. He could attack.

For a split second, when the show led to a commercial with a brief silence in-between, Loretta heard her front door knocking. It startled her, since visitors were uncommon. And it couldn't be Ethan, since, well, he was in the basement.

She stood up and gingerly approached the door, looking through the peephole. Two cops were standing on the porch, both staring at the door, their eyebrows stitched together. There was no doubt they could hear the TV, so the younger cop put a fist together and banged on the door. The older one looked at him and gave a crooked smile.

The younger one, Will Russell, visited the bakery just today and had looked at her with curious eyes.

Fear coursed through her veins. Did someone report Ethan missing? Was she in trouble? Most importantly, how dare they interrupt her watching her favorite show, now that it was getting heated.

She removed her hair from her face, a nervous reaction, and observed the two cops looking at her with curiosity in their eyes. She opened the door to greet the two intruders.

"Good evening. Are you Loretta Davis?" asked the older of the two.

She nodded.

"We're investigating the murder of Amy White." Pause. "You have been reported as a suspect in the murder case."

She widened her eyes and snapped her head back. "What?"

While relief that they weren't here for Ethan washed

over her, a bolt of shock went through her. Why would anyone suspect her to be the murderer if she had nothing to do with it? What evidence did they have to make such a claim?

"We have a few questions for you." The chief raised his voice to compete against the TV. "Can we come in?"

She turned around to look over her shoulder and considered his question. There were a couple of issues. One, Ethan was in the basement, and he would most likely start screaming to be let out at hearing the cops' voices. And two, she was innocent, as simple as that, and she didn't want the cops probing further.

Loretta's head snapped at first, then it violently shook. She yelled, "I didn't do it. I didn't do it! No, no, no!"

Her gaze lost its focus. She zoned out and could no longer see the forest through the trees. She squatted down and buried her face in her legs. Her voice was muffled while she kept yelling.

The Chief approached her and grabbed her by the arm. "Stand up. You're coming with us."

He half-dragged her across the porch, and she nearly fell as she descended the stairs. As they walked away from the house, she could still hear the voices projecting from the TV, mixed with the loud crickets chirping from the nearby woods. Loretta kept up with their stride while ripping herself out of the chief's claws. The chief gripped her arm, as if afraid she could escape. Loretta felt the sharp pain in her arm, and she wanted to scream, but it would do more damage than good if she did. Who would hear her, anyway? Her heart thumped in her chest.

"Let me go." Her voice was barely above a whisper. But Chief Blake paid her no attention and put her in the back seat of the police car.

Loretta gazed at her house helplessly, wondering where they were taking her. She felt terrified. She grabbed her left hand with the other to control the shaking. Tears welled up in her eyes as the town blurred at the speed of the car.

There was no need for the police siren, but it was blasting through the night, amplifying Loretta's fear. They wanted to break her. Make her weaker than she was.

CHAPTER 18

ETHAN WAS PISSED.

It had been over twenty hours since Loretta locked him in the basement. Not only did she refuse to let him out, but now he had to contend with the TV's max volume that he could hear all the way through the basement.

It was unbearable.

He had searched for tools to smash the door, but there was nothing in sight. He turned every single object in his periphery, but there was absolutely nothing. He'd hoped to find an axe or a knife or a metal rod he could use, but not even a tiny Swiss knife. Most of those tools were held in the outside shed, so he was not surprised. He was at her mercy and could only wait for her to come to her senses and open the door.

Did she forget to take her meds today? All sorts of thoughts and questions crossed Ethan's mind, but one was sticking: she would fucking pay for this. He could no longer tolerate her bullshit and live with her weird behavior. And he should really reconsider that dating app he'd met her on. Date Dazzle, or whatever the hell it was called. Her photo was so alluring when he came across her profile, but if he'd known how strange she was, he would have scrolled right past it.

It was already past midnight, and the TV was still at a full blast. Did Loretta leave it on intentionally to stop him going to sleep? If she did, it worked.

He'd been unsuccessful in his dating adventures. Though he wasn't quite the best boyfriend. Once a relationship took over his life, it felt like a large rock had dropped on his chest and he could no longer breathe. Now that he was reaching mid-thirties, it was imperative he settled down, but he wasn't the man to sacrifice.

Dating Loretta was fun at her first, and her little "punishments" were cute. But this—this was out of hand, and it made him regret his choices. How stupid was he to fall for her? Pretty stupid.

He lay down on the couch, covering his forehead with his arm and staring at the ceiling. All the anger he'd felt previously was replaced with dread and disdain. This basement felt like a prison, and his psyche was playing tricks on him. A flicker of rage and revenge ignited inside him, and he wondered how far it would carry. Not that he wanted to harm Loretta, but rage could make people do unexpected things.

Ones he could regret later.

He was fully awake, though he was getting weaker from not using his muscles like he usually did. Running five miles every morning was nothing for Ethan, and he already missed his daily routine. In fact, he was super familiar with the Bearsden Forest conservation. When he first moved to Massachusetts, he explored different areas, and the conservation was his top choice when it came to hiking or running. He'd hike miles and miles on a given day, and look at him now? It felt like he was rotting in Loretta's basement.

It was outrageous of Loretta to do this to him. He wouldn't let her get away with this crap. Never again.

As anger rose up his spine again, he let out a loud scream, deafening his ears. His voice vibrated through the basement, filling his undeniable agony.

Take that, bitch!

He lay back down, feeling spent and hoping he'd awaken Loretta's curiosity, so she'd run to open the door. But even with this loud, desperate scream, Loretta was still unresponsive.

And there was no way out.

CHAPTER 19

DESPITE CHIEF BLAKE'S order to leave the car, Loretta stayed quiet and unresponsive. She stared ahead with her giant eyes, looking at God knew what. Chief Blake didn't have a choice but to grab her arm and drag her out.

"Let's go." He felt this might be a long night as they interrogated her. Her behavior was surely unusual. Being defensive might be the first sign she had something sinister to hide. He hoped they'd get to the bottom of it soon.

The interrogation room was just down the hall. She shuffled behind Chief Blake as he led her. Officer Russell was right behind, ready to tackle this. In fact, he seemed excited, like a small child would be when he received a new toy.

Once in the room, Chief Blake said his spiel about the suspect's right to remain silent as Loretta stared at a spot in front of her. Even though she looked somewhat disheveled, unprepared to end up in the police station tonight, her facial features were beautiful and stood out. She wore a camisole, no bra, and the cold room air hardened her nipples. Her shoulders looked as if they'd been sculpted by a master; her arms, soft hands, and long fingers could serve her well as a watch model. Intricate beauty.

Too bad she was batshit crazy.

Chief Blake tried hard to divert his eyes from her body, but they kept landing on the same spot. Her chest. He forced himself to look at her face and concentrate on what he was about to do. Interrogate.

The small interrogation room was a little too cold for his liking. He understood why. It was akin to a library being cold, so that people reading inside wouldn't fall asleep. Or, in this case, it would make people confess sooner, so they didn't need to contend with such harsh conditions. The air-conditioning in their office was central; there was no way to control it. So, he'd speed up the process and get her to confess quickly.

"Where were you two nights ago?"

Loretta sat still in her chair, her posture perfectly straight, as if she were being propped up by a stick. She appeared more like a mannequin than a living being. Between the car ride and sitting in that chair, something had changed in Loretta. Something snapped, and she was no longer the manic, hyperactive woman, but a quiet, reserved one with empty eyes. She looked like she was in a trance, hypnotized.

A minute later, Chief Blake repeated the question. "Can you tell us where you were two nights ago?"

The officer gazed at the two cameras occasionally. He

looked nervous and out of place, as if wishing these cameras weren't plastered to the wall.

Time ticked away, and Loretta continued her silence.

The two would occasionally look at each other, unsure of what to do. Loretta wouldn't say a word, and it was frustrating Chief Blake. He'd dealt with uncooperative suspects in petty crimes before, but there was something unsettling about Loretta's demeanor that unnerved him.

"Look, Loretta," Chief Blake started again, his patience wearing thin. "We know you were seen near the scene of the crime. We have witnesses who saw you there. Now, we just need to know what you were doing."

Chief Blake used his proven tactic to get people to confess. He lied. He wished there were witnesses. All of this would be easier.

Still, Loretta remained silent, her expression unchanged. Chief Blake exchanged a glance with Officer Russell, who shrugged helplessly.

"Okay, if you won't talk, we'll have to go through this the hard way," Chief Blake said, his tone firm. "We can hold you here until you decide to cooperate. It's in your best interest to talk."

He sat down and leaned back in his chair, studying Loretta's face for any sign of reaction. But she remained impassive, as though she were made of stone.

As the minutes ticked by, the atmosphere in the room grew tense. Chief Blake could feel the weight of the unanswered questions pressing down on him. He glanced at the clock on the wall, willing time to move faster.

Suddenly, Loretta's lips parted, and she spoke, her voice barely above a whisper. "I was there," she said, her words sending a shiver down Chief Blake's spine. "But I didn't do anything."

Chief Blake leaned forward; his interest piqued. "What do you mean, you were there? What were you doing?"

Loretta hesitated. Her gaze fixed on some distant point beyond the walls of the interrogation room. "I was just . . . watching," she said finally. "I wanted to see."

Chief Blake exchanged a puzzled glance with Officer Russell. "See what?"

Loretta shook her head, a hint of sadness flickering in her eyes. "I can't tell you," she whispered. "You wouldn't understand."

Frustration bubbled up inside the chief. He had hoped for a breakthrough, but it seemed they were no closer to unraveling the mystery surrounding Loretta. He couldn't tell if she was telling the truth, but if he ventured a guess, they weren't any closer to it. She obviously wasn't in touch with reality, and she was just spewing delusions from her head. There was no way she was watching Amy getting murdered. There wasn't even a speck of conviction in her voice. Loretta was losing it. Entering her depressive phase. The bubbly Loretta had vanished.

Consulting a psychologist to evaluate her would help determine if she was fit to be questioned.

Chief Blake didn't know how to deal with the woman. He finished questioning her for now. Maybe the homicide detective, who was starting tomorrow, bright and early, would have more luck.

"Fine," he said, his voice tinged with irritation. "But you're not leaving here until we get more answers."

With that, Chief Blake signaled to Officer Russell, and they both rose from their seats, leaving Loretta alone in the dimly lit room. As they stepped out into the corridor, Chief Blake couldn't shake the feeling that they were only scratching the surface of something much darker and more sinister than they had imagined. And until they uncovered the truth, Loretta would remain a puzzle they were determined to solve.

CHAPTER 20

SARAH ELMWOOD WOKE up at six a.m., as usual. It was a healthy habit since her college days. Her mind worked best in the early hours.

She liked her daily routine: making coffee, watching the news, taking her dog, Koko, out for a walk. She didn't mind her solitary life, especially since she was always surrounded by people in the city. Somerville was one of the most populated cities in Massachusetts, if not the country, with houses so close to each other you could open the window and stretch to touch the neighboring house.

She liked Somerville. It inspired her to write novels in an urban setting. She could spend all day at her desk, writing, writing, writing, and then just step outside and be in the middle of hustle and bustle.

Athol, where she grew up, was so different. It was more tamed and friendlier.

The morning news about the murder shocked her. That was a first.

Amy White.

Sarah almost dropped her mug of coffee all over the living room couch when she saw the young woman's photo appear on TV.

Any news about her town was an anomaly, so she felt a jolt of unease as she watched the screen, her mind racing with questions. Who would want to harm Amy, a familiar face in their close-knit community? And more importantly, could it happen again? As the details unfolded, Sarah couldn't shake off the chilling realization that the tranquility of their town was shattered, leaving behind a lingering sense of vulnerability. She took a deep breath, steeling herself for whatever lay ahead.

Her family no longer lived in Athol. Her father had died when she was a teenager, and her mom remarried and moved to Colorado ten years later. Her younger brother was in the Army and often served overseas. Sarah was the only one who'd stayed in Massachusetts after her father's death.

Now she only had Koko.

As soon as she heard of the murder, her childhood friend Loretta came to her mind immediately. Last time they texted wasn't that long ago. Sarah was dying to know more about the murder, and who else to ask but people who lived in the town? Besides, Loretta's father had asked Sarah to keep an eye out on his daughter, to remain friends with her, and to check on her occasionally, when he was gone. Which she had, though they rarely saw each other anymore.

She texted her as soon as she heard the news of the murder. She expected a speedy response—within minutes—which was often the case with Loretta. But not today. An hour later, Sarah's text remained unanswered, and a flicker of concern ignited inside her.

At nine a.m., there was still no response from Loretta.

A surprise visit was in order.

Sarah poured coffee into a mug and secured it with a lid. She put Koko in the back of her car, anxiety coursing through her. What could keep Loretta from answering her text? Besides writing, she had nothing else to do that day. She could use a quick break from her characters.

As she drove on Route 2, heading west, the traffic thinned, and the trees thickened as she progressed toward the destination. Sometimes she missed the tranquility of suburbs. She opened her window to enjoy the fresh air coming in. Koko was in the back, her nose sticking out through the small window opening. Sarah turned the music on and bobbed her head at the beat.

Why would Loretta remain silent for so long? Was something wrong? As she steered the wheel, she gazed at her phone occasionally to check if Loretta responded. But there was nothing. She hoped she was just busy with something.

Due to her bi-polar, Loretta had been prone to harming herself since they were teenagers. In the back of Sarah's mind, she wondered if she'd ever harm another human being. But Sarah had always felt safe around her.

Except that one time.

They were still in high school, and Loretta had a crush on a boy who ended up asking Sarah out. Upon hearing Sarah's revelation, Loretta stood immobile and gave her friend a piercing look. Then she'd slapped Sarah hard, causing her head to jerk to the side. She'd come out of her haunting stupor as if a devil had taken over her body, then left as soon as she struck Sarah. For the rest of the day, Loretta kept apologizing, saying she didn't mean to do what she did, and she never would do it. Sarah believed her. And promptly forgave her. It was probably surprising that she was still friends with Loretta, since they had nothing in common, but a promise was a promise.

The town looked the same as the last time she came to visit it a few years ago. She didn't venture there often unless she had to. The only difference this time was that it seemed quiet and ghostly, as if a veil of fear covered it. It had to be the effect of the recent murder.

Sarah drove down the path leading to Loretta's house and immediately noticed the Jeep sitting on the side of the road. It looked like Loretta had visitors. Could it be her new boyfriend? If so, she hadn't told her a thing about him. She sped up a little until she arrived at the house and parked on the side. The house looked the same as before, except the façade looked choppier.

At a near distance, a cow mooed, so she walked to the barn to check up on the animals. The cow was pacing around the pen, its tail moving viciously, signaling its agitation. The chickens nearby hopped and skipped, cackling like crazy. They could sense something was different.

They could sense the absence of normalcy around here. The sounds sent an unsettling vibe.

Koko stood in the same spot, her ears like antennas pointing at the house. She seemed hesitant to move forward, but Sarah nudged her with the leash and said, "Come on, let's go."

She barked toward the house, desperately trying to get herself off the leash. Sarah took caution. She pulled Koko closer and patted her on the head. "It's okay, baby. It's okay."

She'd hoped Loretta would suddenly emerge from the house and greet her, but she didn't. She heard a loud noise coming from the house, albeit muffled by the walls. It sounded like a radio or TV, but she couldn't be sure.

The door was unlocked. Her heart thumped as she slowly opened the door. It was as if an unspoken danger lurked from behind. The dog whimpered and struggled to escape, but Sarah kept her close, pulling on her leash.

As soon as the door was open, the loud noise projected through the air. The TV was on. Sarah cringed at just how loud it was. She found the TV remote and turned it off. The eerie silence replaced the loud noise, heightening her senses.

Where was Loretta? Why did she leave the TV on, and why wasn't she coming to greet her? Her green Subaru was parked in front of the house, and she seemed to have a guest. But the house seemed empty.

Just as she ascended the stairs to look for her in the bedroom, a big thump coming from the main floor startled her. Koko barked at the noise and pulled Sarah toward the basement door.

"Open the door!"

Sarah heard the male's voice, but she didn't recognize it.

"Who are you?" Sarah asked.

"Come on, open the door, I'm begging you!"

Koko kept barking while Sarah tried to control her, unsuccessfully. Was Loretta in there with the man? Perhaps they'd somehow locked themselves in and couldn't get out.

She reached for the knob, but the door wouldn't budge.

"The door is locked." Sarah said, as she looked around searching for something.

"The key. There's a key somewhere," the angry voice from behind the door said.

Sarah turned around and frantically started searching for the key. Where the hell would the basement key be held? It could be anywhere. But she supposed the most commonplace would be the hallway.

She walked to the dresser and opened all the drawers, but there were no keys. The man behind the door wouldn't stop banging on it, so Sarah was getting annoyed.

"I can't find the key!" she sounded desperate.

"Check the kitchen!"

She ran to the kitchen, where a foul odor splashed her. Ugh. It had to be spoiled milk or something that didn't get properly refrigerated. She gagged and blocked her nose, controlling her urge not to throw up. Then, a sliver of hope washed over her when she saw a single key sitting on the kitchen table. She grabbed it and ran to the door, placing the key inside the slot, fearing what she might come across as soon as the door opened.

A young, handsome man appeared on the other side of the door with anger etched on his face. Koko barked, propping her paws, trying to sniff the man. Bite him?

Sarah studied him. "Who are you?"

But he didn't respond. He frantically walked around the house, grabbing all his possessions: his phone, his backpack, his flannel shirt hanging on the hook in the hallway. His brows were creased while he focused on getting out of there as soon as he could. Koko barked at him, but the man didn't give two shits. He was getting out of dodge.

"Hey, where's Loretta?" Sarah stood in the same spot, watching him gather his stuff.

He stopped momentarily and looked at her. "How the hell should I know?" he screamed.

He stormed out of the house and slammed the door behind. Sarah walked to the window and observed the man hasten to his Jeep, then the dust flew in the air as he drove away.

All this puzzled Sarah. And none of it answered her questions about where Loretta was.

She walked down to the basement to see if she could be there, but the space was empty.

Maybe she should stick around until she showed up? But then she checked the clock and panicked when she remembered the weekly meeting with her agent was today, and it was going to start in exactly an hour.

Shit!

Her ride to Somerville could take longer than that, so she better leave now. Loretta, she hoped, was fine, though it worried her to see the unknown man in her house, all fired up about something. Sure, none of this made sense, but deep down, Sarah felt Loretta was fine. It wasn't the first time she'd done something stupid, which, locking this guy in the basement, clearly was.

She pulled her phone out of her pocket to text her agent:

> Hey, I may be a few minutes late, but I will see you soon.

Their meetings always took place on Zoom, because her agent lived in New York City. Just as she rushed through the door, she paused and looked around one more time. Maybe she should send Loretta another text and let her know she came to see her.

She opened her phone and quickly typed up a message:

> Hey, I came to see you, but you weren't home. And btw, I just released the Hulk from your basement. Haha

Then she stormed out of the house, put Koko in the back seat, and drove away without looking back.

CHAPTER 21

OFFICER RUSSELL HAD a perfect theory about Loretta Davis.

And he couldn't wait to share it with the newly assigned homicide detective, Shawn Bradley. He was joining their small team today.

They'd scheduled a briefing with him at one in the afternoon, but since the officer was up all night, combing through records and forming his theories, he'd better go home and get some sleep. He was quite tired, and he didn't want to lose his smile. He was sure he'd impress both the chief and the detective with how he'd tied the events to the prime suspect. Apparently, Loretta had a motive. Whether it was she who killed Amy or hired someone to do it, she was the mastermind behind all this.

Besides, in Officer Russell's eyes, she'd acted guilty when they questioned her. Very guilty. Now that he had probed into her records and her past more, there was no doubt she was involved. As he drove home, he recited a speech, a briefing in his head, to Detective Bradley and Chief Blake. In his mind, he envisioned himself remaining perfectly motionless, wearing a poker face, to convey the seriousness and professionalism that would accompany his delivery of findings. He couldn't wait.

That afternoon, Officer Russell powered through the police station and entered the conference room, where the briefing took place. Detective Bradley, a rather large man with wide shoulders and salt-and-pepper hair, was sitting at the table and chatting with Chief Blake. The officer's palms sweated, but he did his best to regulate his nerves and show confidence. Now was the time to impress his superiors.

After brief introductions and a niceties exchange, the detective dove right in. "So, tell me about this murder case."

Chief Blake and Officer Russell gazed at each other, as if they were deciding who should speak. With Chief Blake's nod, the officer got the green light, so he turned to face Detective Bradley and started from the top.

Detective Bradley's brows creased as he tentatively listened to all the evidence gathered so far. The officer could tell what he was thinking. Not much. A bloody knife confirmed to have been used to kill Amy White, but other than that, nothing. One prime suspect? A mentally unstable woman?

"Who have you interviewed so far?" he said.

"Amy's husband, Andy, who had a perfect alibi. No

way he was involved," the officer said. "We interviewed his mother, and they're both clean."

"Okay." The detective put his elbow on the chair to support his face in his hand. "Go on."

"We've also interviewed Amy's neighbors, and they didn't help much at all. A couple of them said they'd seen Amy the day before she died, but that was it." He shrugged. "Liz and Bob, the bakery owners, are clean, too."

"We're still waiting for the DNA results on the knife, but I've dug some records of our suspect, and I'm led to believe there is high likeliness that she was involved in the murder."

The detective raised his brows in surprise and tilted his head as if the officer was saying gibberish.

"According to her records, she has been institutionalized several times for obstructing peace in public places and for assault and battery. She is diagnosed with bipolar and, in fact, has been institutionalized several times. According to her records, she has battled with both depression and psychosis and has suffered delusions ... and a slew of other things."

"Delusions? Like what?"

The following piece of information led Officer Russell to form his theory that Loretta's craziness and her past led to murder. This was it. They'd both better listen well.

"She has believed in the past that she was pregnant and wore a fake pregnancy belly to convince others. You know, a silicon one? You can buy a used one on Amazon real cheap. She showed up at the hospital to deliver the baby, then believed that she had stillborn." The officer swallowed a chunk stuck in his throat. He cleared before he could continue. "The nurse who supposedly delivered her baby was Amy White. So, after she believed she lost her baby, she assaulted the nurse. Killed her."

There was heavy silence in the room. Chief Blake and Detective Bradley were taking the time to digest the information. The detective's eyes widened, and he put his arm down and straightened in his chair, leaning forward. "So, you believe our suspect killed the nurse for revenge?"

"That's what I believe, yes. She had a motive."

"Did you search her place?"

"Yes."

They had sought a search warrant and flipped the house inside out, searching for any evidence leading to Amy White's murder. But nothing conclusive was found.

"But we're still waiting to get the lab results, right?"

"Yes."

"What else do we know about the suspect? Is she married? Who does she live with?"

The officer lowered his eyes and scratched his nose before his gaze landed on the detective. "No, she's not married. She lives alone, at least according to the records."

A mentally unstable woman in her thirties. They somehow didn't fare well in society. They were neither here nor there. Not young enough to be excused for not marrying and having children, yet not old enough to avoid a judgment for her choices. A curse of middle age. A woman like Loretta became a spinster and lived a lonely life until she died, unaware of how odd she really was. Perhaps she'd be lucky enough to find her own cocoon and stay out of trouble. Loretta was still searching for hers, it seemed.

Officer Russell still knew that if the bloody knife didn't deliver conclusive evidence, all this could be for nothing. Their only hope then would be for her to confess under pressure.

"Where is she now?" Detective Bradley asked.

"She's still in custody. She has spoken very little since we brought her to the police station. I mean, she said a few things that made no sense, but nothing we can use."

"How long has it been?"

The officer gazed at his watch. "Less than twenty-four hours. Be my guest and question her more."

"Lead me to her." The detective stood up and headed for the door.

Chief Blake seemed pleased with the officer's work. He gave Officer Russell a quick smile when Detective Bradley exited the room.

By six o'clock in the evening, the forensic lab released the DNA test results of the bloody knife. They confirmed the blood found on the knife belonged to Amy White, but there was absolutely nothing else—no other physical evidence or fingerprints—to confirm their prime suspect was the murderer.

"Shit." Chief Blake involuntarily let the swear word out as they combed through the report.

"Now what?" the officer asked.

"Well, we don't have enough evidence Loretta was ever involved in the murder," Detective Bradley added. He scratched his head. "We can't hold her in custody anymore. So, let her go, but keep a close eye on her."

Officer Russell felt like a large stone fell on his heart. He thought he'd got to the bottom of it all, but clearly there was more work to be done. Nothing was as easy as it seemed.

He took Loretta by the arm and led her through the police station hallway, feeling pissed. He squeezed Loretta's arm so hard that she yelped. He could apologize if the bitch hadn't done a good job of ruining his chance for a promotion and moving on with his life. Surely, he could give her a ride home, but he chose not to. Fuck that. He had better things to do.

CHAPTER 22

WHEN LORETTA EMERGED from the police station, she had the surreal feeling of being deposited on an unfamiliar planet. That entire experience inside had taken her on a wild ride. The police questioning her, probing into her past, assuming she was the one who killed Amy. It was all so weird.

The brightness outside, a stark difference between the dark room in the police station, made her squint. It was too much to handle.

She stood in the parking lot and closed her eyes, soaking up the sounds of traffic on the main street. She felt disoriented even though she'd passed by the police station a zillion times before, and her house wasn't far from the location. Two miles at the most. A deep inhale made her dizzy. She smelled the sweet aroma of pine trees nearby, causing her stomach to growl.

She couldn't wait to get home, eat, and take a shower.

And rest. Two miles used to be nothing just a few short days ago, but now they seemed like a chore.

Her movement was slow. She shuffled down the path, reflecting on what had happened in the past day. How did she become the prime suspect in the murder case of Amy White? Was it something she'd done to draw attention?

And her memory could be fragile. It played tricks on her mind, blurring the line between reality and her imagination. Sometimes, she would distort negative occurrences in her mind and push them to the periphery of her consciousness to avoid being constantly reminded of them. But she was almost sure she didn't kill Amy. It was because Amy was killed roughly two days ago, and all Loretta did at the time was clean her house.

Ethan came into her mind. She'd locked him up for how many days now? She'd lost track. He had to be on the edge, patiently awaiting to be released. Well, what did he expect when he was being incompliant? Infiltrating and sneaking into her bed was not part of the rules. Yet, she decided she'd release him as soon as she arrived home. At least he wasn't cold or starving. His situation was a lot more pleasant than being detained at the police station for a whole day.

But she realized her punishment was too harsh. She'd never kept Ethan—or anyone else, for that matter—in the basement longer than a few hours. When time was up, they'd learned their lesson, and things improved. But keeping someone in the basement for days was a crime. Surely, she didn't mean for that to happen.

Darkness was quickly settling on the horizon, making Loretta hasten her steps before it got too dark. Where she lived, there were no lampposts, and it was difficult to follow the path in the thick woods. She was empty-handed, with nothing to aid her vision. Her phone was tucked between the couch cushions in the living room, where she'd accidentally placed it while watching TV. It would be a welcome tool to light the path in front of her.

All she wanted was to get home as soon as possible.

As she advanced toward her house, heavy steps trudged right from behind, following her, competing with the birds chirping on the nearby tree. This location was always questionable; when Loretta was young, her father would tell her to avoid it, because local thugs threatened the innocent for petty change. Before she turned around to see who'd followed her, the wind was knocked out of her lungs.

Her blood turned to ice in her veins as someone grabbed her from behind and placed a bag over her head.

Fear filled every part of her as she choked on the darkness in front of her face.

The grip was tight, and Loretta had no strength to peel herself away from the intruder. In an attempt at freedom, she desperately tried to pry his hands off, but they were big, calloused, and clung to Loretta like a ravenous hawk ready to devour its prey. The hands had to belong to a large man. A villainous man.

Panic took over. There was no air, no matter how hard she gasped. She was going to die.

She grunted and wanted to scream as loudly as possible, but she couldn't breathe. Her feet dangled helplessly off the ground, and her arms reached for the offender, but they felt like jello, unable to grasp anything.

What was happening? Why would someone want to abduct her? Maybe even kill her? If the bag didn't get removed from her head, she was going to pass out soon.

There was something in that bag, some kind of substance, that was making her incredibly sleepy. Her eyes rolled about in her sockets while she fought the sleepiness. Struggling to stay awake, she briefly questioned if she was on the verge of death.

She mustered all her strength and fought fiercely, despite being on the verge of losing consciousness. The battle was lost. The captor had her, and there was nothing she could do to free herself.

Her captor propped her on his shoulder, with her stomach resting on top of it, and carried her with hasty movements. The only thing that kept her awake was a sharp pain coursing through her belly. Seconds later, her body got dropped on a hard surface. It felt like the trunk of a car, but she couldn't verify. Everything seemed so hazy, as if she had entered a bad dream. She descended into a dark hole, completely losing her bearings.

CHAPTER 23

LIZ TOOK a rag from the sink and wiped the countertop, which was typically Loretta's job. But now she was reduced to doing more, amounting to these thankless tasks, because their employee was ... what? A murderer?

"How many times did I tell you we should let her go? How many?" She stopped wiping for a few seconds then resumed with the same force.

Bob, standing nearby, pinched his nose as if contemplating how things could have gone so wrong with Loretta.

Bob looked at Liz and nodded. "I'm not surprised, though. Everything she went through recently."

"Like what?" Liz scoffed. "Her life isn't any harder than any of ours."

Bob cocked his head and made a face. "Come on, Liz. If you lost a child, you'd probably be a wreck yourself."

Liz put her hands on her waist and pursed her lips. "You still believe she had a stillborn? Don't be a fool, Bob."

Bob widened his eyes at her. "Seriously, Liz? Didn't you see her pregnant? Are you kidding me right now?"

She leaned forward, while her hands still rested on her waist, and raised her voice. "She wasn't pregnant! Her belly didn't carry a baby! That was all fake. Fake, fake, fake."

"How can someone fake pregnancy?" Bob sounded genuinely confused.

"She wore an artificial pregnancy belly. To fool everyone." She brought her index finger to her temple and swirled it around, then whistled. "Yeah, she's that crazy. Everyone in town knows and calls her Crazy Loretta."

Liz smirked. Bob would at least now finally see all the truth about *his* Loretta. That she wasn't this sweet little thing, but a witch who used her good looks as a tool to manipulate.

Fuck them both.

Bob shook his head. "I don't know. Something still doesn't seem right."

"What doesn't seem right?"

"The fake pregnancy. Her being the prime suspect of the murder. I mean, she never struck me as a killer, as strange as she might be."

"Oh, Bob. You're so blind and smitten by her. But I know her type. She's dangerous."

"What type?" Bob said. Liz just waved her hand as a response. "What should we do about this place now?" His eyes darted all over the bakery, as if dreading what was to come.

"What do you mean?"

"Well, our customers enjoyed visiting and talking to Loretta, whether you like that or not. Now that she's the prime suspect, who would want to come visit?

"I'm not too worried," Liz said. "People like to talk, visit places where a murder took place. Or where a murderer worked."

"Give me a break," Bob protested. "People are filled with fear, worried that they might be the next target."

Liz pondered his statement, then shook her head. "No, I don't think so. People just love drama. They like to be in the middle of it as much as they fear it."

"So, what are you saying?"

"Well, I don't think we're going to lose any customers, if that's what you're hinting. If anything, they will come over to find out updates about Loretta or see what's going on with the case."

Bob shook his head and placed a hand on his temple.

"Liz, I'm leaving."

She was somewhere in the back. The store had already opened, ready for customers.

Liz emerged from behind the wall and said, "Where are you going? I need you!"

"I just need to clear my head. I'll be back."

"Bob!" Liz sounded desperate. "Bob!"

CHAPTER 24

LORETTA WOKE up to a sharp pain throbbing in her head.

The last thing she remembered was being thrown into a car trunk, with the engine revving towards an unknown destination. Then everything turned black. She must have passed out en route to whatever this place was.

When she peeled her eyes open, she scrutinized her surroundings with deep confusion. Where was she? Despite the perplexing circumstances, she found the strength to smile, grateful for her survival.

She lay on what felt like an overused, thin mattress. The air was thick with mold, dust, and age. The location resembled a dilapidated cabin, showing signs of rust and neglect from years of disuse. A lone and what appeared as a malfunctioning light bulb hung from a string attached to the ceiling.

Loretta's mouth was dry and parched. She was dying

for a glass of water. Food would be nice, too, but hunger wasn't as distracting as the thirst.

She eased the stabbing pain by resting her head on her hands and softly massaging her temples. As she rubbed against the skin, a metallic aroma reached her nose.

Dried blood.

The tips of her fingers were deep crimson. She ran over her head with her hands and felt a bump. Between physical fatigue, hunger, and thirst, she could tolerate the pain a lot better. Her hair was disheveled, and the smeared blood got her hair stuck to her skull like glue.

A warm bath would be nice, but she had a hunch she was nowhere near a functional bathroom with hot water.

The room she occupied was tiny, and the walls were made of wooden panels. The floor was covered in wooden planks, old and dusty from the surrounding forest. The bed was naked, with no pillows or blankets, so she suspected she'd get cold with only a camisole on if she ended up sleeping here, especially now that summer was on its way out.

There was nothing else in the room besides the bed. The absence of furniture revealed marks and faded carpet on the floor. The window, once perhaps a source of natural light, now stood opaque with grime, casting eerie shadows across the desolate space. The walls whispered tales of neglect and abandonment. The room was silent, with only the occasional murmurs from the outside. The place seemed to mourn its forgotten past.

Dead silence. That thought filled Loretta with dread. If she screamed, how far would her voice reach? Would anyone hear her?

Convinced that the cabin was secluded, she could only hear the calls of nature from the outside.

The air smelled of mold and old wood, making it difficult to breathe. When Loretta was a child, she had asthma, rendering her helpless during major attacks. Her lungs had felt heavy, as if someone had dropped rocks on her chest. Although her asthma dwindled over the years, as her lungs expanded with age, she felt the heaviness of the air. It made her yearn for her old inhaler, wary and scared her asthma would return.

Maybe her stay here, for whatever reason, was just temporary. Whoever brought her here must have made a mistake and would let her out soon. If they believed she had something to do with Amy's murder, they were wrong.

She spotted an inconspicuous window on one side of the wall. It was hard to notice at first, as it blended with the wall and was covered in spiderwebs and old, dried leaves. She wanted to take a better look outside, so she got off the bed and shuffled over to it. She fell to the floor with a thud, her hands becoming bloody as they met with a sharp splinter.

"Damn it," she whispered.

She turned around and noticed a thick chain across the floor, a link on one side tied to her ankle. The other side was secured to the wall, with no chance of freeing it. The chain was only five feet long, long enough to allow Loretta to move in and around the bed, but not long enough to walk to the window and peek through to study her new location.

Or to get to the door, which was probably secured with a lock on the other side.

There was no question she was a prisoner. But why and by whom, she couldn't even guess.

Fear was the only thing she felt now.

While sitting on the floor, her eyes bulged from the effort of trying to see through the window. Despite the thick dust on the glass, she was sure she could see thick trees with branches swaying against the clouds. It was difficult to know what time of day it was, as the trees cast a heavy shadow over everything.

She couldn't figure out the reasons behind her confinement in this dingy place. The only thing her mind focused on was how she was going to get out of here. Even in the high-stake situation, she thought of Ethan and how he was still locked up in the basement. Funny how they both ended up locked in at someone's mercy. She wanted to get out of here, so she could free him. She'd prolonged Ethan's capture, and she didn't mean to punish him so severely.

But a flicker of doubt ignited in her mind.

Maybe someone had already found him and set him free.

Maybe Ethan broke the door and fled.

Maybe it was he who'd found her and locked her in the cabin.

Maybe it was Ethan's turn to teach her a lesson. Because maybe she most definitely deserved it.

CHAPTER 25

LATER THAT DAY, Chief Blake and Officer Russell patrolled around the town in the police car. Most of the time, the town looked uneventful, like today. They planned to grab lunch at a nearby town and kill the time.

They briefly discussed meeting Detective Bradley.

"He's an excellent addition to our team," Chief Blake pointed out. In the back of his mind, he was picturing his feet up on the ottoman and TV on in front of him. His life had come down to that. Every minute spent at work made him realize how tired he was; how time stretched into infinity.

"Yeah," Officer Russell agreed. "Sounds like he's digging it."

Digging it?

Chief Blake didn't bother asking what he meant, so he let it go.

"You did a lot of work on the case, huh?"

Officer Russell gave him a proud smile. It was like he'd waited for someone to get murdered all these years, so he could finally put his actual skill to the test. "Once you start digging, it gets easier. Believe me."

Chief Blake nodded. He had a hunch.

Even though Officer Russell had dug up a lot of dirt on Loretta, they were still far from solving the case. Loretta Davis needed a psychiatric evaluation to determine her state of mind. For crying out loud, they couldn't even interrogate her or get information out of her without questioning her sanity. They couldn't lock her up, either, since there was no conclusive evidence she was involved in the murder.

Thankfully, Detective Bradley was an experienced homicide detective. This was not his first rodeo. But Chief Blake couldn't help but notice doubt flickering in his eyes during the briefing. Did he believe they lacked the size and experience to help solve the case? Did he view them with contempt?

What the hell did he care?

As Chief Blake drove, he turned to Officer Russell. "So, this gal Loretta..."

Officer Russell jerked his head toward the Chief, "Yes?"

"... this Loretta gal. Do you know her from before?" Chief Blake inquired.

"Yeah," Officer Russell said. "I actually do."

"I thought so. You seem to be of a similar age."

"I know her from high school."

"Is that right?"

"Yeah. She was ... how should I say this?" Officer Russell looked for an appropriate description. "Super weird."

"Yeah? How?"

"She used to hit and yell at people out of the blue. Apparently, she was diagnosed with bi-polar, but none of us knew. We just assumed she hated the world."

Chief Blake gazed at Officer Russell; his forehead creased. "Did she do anything to show it?"

"Yeah, I mean, she would just come out of the building, stand in the middle of the baseball field and scream with her eyes closed."

"Huh. Was she screaming at someone in particular?"

"Nope. Just out in the air. We called her Crazy Loretta. Her tantrums became excessive at some point. She'd do something strange every other day." Officer Russell let out a nervous chuckle.

"Too bad," Chief Blake said. "She's a beautiful woman." The chief's hand travelled absentmindedly to his balls, and he gave them a discrete rub.

"Did you ever ask her out?"

"What?" Officer Russell jerked his head toward the chief.

"Back in high school...did you ever ask her out?"

"God, no." Officer Russell sighed as he rubbed his nose. "Yeah, she was hot and all, but it was difficult to talk to her. She wasn't that approachable."

"Hm."

"Besides, when she was at her low, she skipped classes and wouldn't show up at school for days." He paused. "I don't know. I think they call it a depressive phase in her disorder or something like that? As crazy as she was, she could also be quiet. She wouldn't talk to anyone."

"Yeah, my wife had bi-polar," Chief Blake admitted. He shook his head slightly as he recalled memories from their marriage and continued, "I loved her, but sometimes she was impossible to stick around. One day wild and full of energy, and the next day, lying in bed and crying all day."

"Really? I'm sorry. I didn't know."

"That's okay. The worst part was that I couldn't help her. She was taking meds, but they helped only a little."

Silence ensued as they hit Route 2, leading to the town next door. Chief Blake sped up hard, gluing them to their seats. When he steadied the speed, he gazed at the officer. "You know, I have a strange feeling that Loretta has nothing to do with this murder."

Officer Russell stared at him, waiting for an explanation.

"One thing I'm good at is reading people, and the more time we spent with her, the more I thought she couldn't have done it." He scratched the back of his neck. "But of course, I could be totally off."

"Yeah, I think you are. Because I can definitely see Loretta doing something like this. You don't know how crazy she really is," Officer Russell insisted. "And how do you explain the knife? Who else could it leave it in the bakery?"

"I suppose that's true."

Officer Russell rolled his eyes as he looked out the window.

CHAPTER 26

AFTER LUNCH AT A RESTAURANT, Officer Russell found himself back in the police station kitchen, pouring himself a hot cup of joe.

Their office assistant, Marybelle, made a new carafe and refilled it every few hours, because that's what the police station needed—to be always caffeinated.

He already thought about going home and relaxing, because he'd been up all night the night before, and fatigue had caught up to him. He pictured himself lounging on the sofa in his living room and watching movies while sipping a beer. His best buddy, Ryan, was in town, and he was dying to see him. But Ryan said he'd be spending time with family the first couple of days.

The Officer could use some company, that was for sure. He didn't have many friends anymore. They all dispersed and left the town for "bigger and better" things. His destiny was to stick around and follow his passion, which was to be a local cop. Shit, maybe he should have chosen another career, so he could travel some more and see the world. But he was anchored to the town, as his ill mother still lived here. He could never leave her behind.

Mary, his mother, suffered from Alzheimer's and lived in the senior living community two towns over. Officer Russell thought she'd be better off being taken care of by people who knew the disease a lot better than him. Some days were quite rough for the officer. He'd go visit his mom, and she couldn't recognize him. She'd stare at him at first, then ask what his name was, how they knew each other. Both annoyance and sadness would fill him. The woman who'd held him in her womb, two hearts so close, now estranged in many ways.

He couldn't quite deal with his mother descending into a black hole, so he visited her less and less over time.

She surely wouldn't care either way. Her disease had overtaken her life, and she was like a vegetable waiting to rot and perish.

Officer Russell texted Ryan to find out if he was free tonight. Any distraction would be good. They could hang out at his place or go to a local bar and catch up. Whatever worked.

A few minutes later, Ryan responded:

> Sorry, but I can't. Something urgent
> came up. I'll be back in a few months.

The Officer made a face, feeling rejected. Even his best buddy didn't have time for him.

He turned around and looked at Marybelle, wondering

if she might be free tonight. She seemed focused on her computer and typing vigorously. If her face wasn't so creased as she concentrated, she'd look a lot more attractive. Well, she was not unattractive. She had long, red hair and full lips, and her curves were an asset. But, if the Officer was being honest with himself, he and Marybelle weren't in the same league. He was a lot more handsome, and she was just average. Besides, she might be in a relationship already, or at the least, dating someone.

In any case, he'd rather spend time alone tonight.

Embarrassed about his idea of taking Marybelle out on a date, with his head hanging low, he walked to his office and sat at his desk.

Chief Blake didn't come to the office today, and, for a second, the officer forgot he had a day off. An urgent family matter.

He stifled a yawn when Detective Bradley stormed in.

"Hey, Will, how's it going?"

His voice was deep and authoritative. The officer used to fear peers resembling the detective when he was younger, but now he was in an authoritative role himself, that fear dissipated.

"Hey. Not bad."

The detective sat down across from the officer and crossed his leg over the other. He sat in silence and gazed at the floor. Did he have something important to announce?

"Well, looks like we may have a break." He rubbed his chin as if he was thinking. "We have a witness saying they might have seen Loretta on the night of the murder, near the murder scene. I think we need to bring her back to the police station and question her more. Until she confesses."

The officer stared at the detective in disbelief. "Who saw her?"

"An anonymous call."

His theory was firming up. He wanted to smile, but it was inappropriate.

"Anonymous?" he repeated, lost for words.

The detective stood up and said, "You know where she lives? Let's go find her."

He followed him like a puppy, excited they were on the case again. His glittering prize came a little closer, and that thought filled his chest with warmth and happiness.

On their way to Loretta's house, the two conducted a small talk.

"So, you like your job?" The detective peeked at the Officer then placed his gaze back on the road again.

"Yeah, I love my job," the Officer said with enthusiasm in his voice.

"Some days are better than others, right?" The detective laughed. His question was rhetorical.

"I guess so." The officer was short.

"So, any kids?" the detective asked.

The officer looked at the detective and said with a whisper, "No kids."

No kids. Not even a girlfriend, for crying out loud. He seemed too tied to his career and didn't do too much about his dating scene, either. Maybe when things settled with the case, he would take a vacation and revisit his life goals. It would be worth it. Because, deep down, he didn't want to grow old.

"How 'bout you?" The officer didn't want this to be all about him.

"Two kids. One boy, one girl. Twins. Almost teenagers," the detective said. "It's crazy how time flies. Before you know it, they plot getting away from responsibilities. Good thing I can read 'em like a book."

"Our calling comes in handy, for sure."

Detective Bradley nodded and laughed. "That's right. But at the end of the day, they're the best. They are who I live for."

The officer tried to hide the envy he felt as the detective boasted about his children. It occurred to him why he was a loner. Avoiding stories of people attaining success through having children, living in a stunning house with a loving family, and never experiencing loneliness was much easier. Maybe it was easier to focus on what he had, mainly a half-baked career, than a family he desired.

They drove onto the gravel road leading to Loretta's house. Little rocks crackled under the tires like a firework. The officer rested his eyes on the house.

The door was wide open.

Strange.

No lights on in the house, even though the darkness settled in the sky like a heavy blanket. A shiver crawled up his spine as he stepped out of the car. Instinctively, his hand moved towards the holster at his hip, a precautionary gesture.

"Stay close," he muttered to his partner, who nodded in agreement. As they cautiously approached the open door, the silence of the night seemed to amplify every creak of the wooden porch beneath their feet. With each step, the sense of unease grew stronger, signaling that something was amiss in Loretta's usually tranquil abode.

They looked at each other and proceeded inside. The detective rested his hand on the pistol.

They gingerly walked around the house, and Officer Russell gagged at the foul odor coming from the kitchen. While the rest of the house looked spotless, a pile of unwashed dishes sat in the sink, the food on them rotting and attracting flies.

"Jesus!" Detective Bradley walked away as soon as he could.

They checked every corner, every nook and cranny, but nothing was there. The house was empty and eerie. The basement door was swung wide open, and the officer stood at the top, contemplating whether he should descend. He decided not to and turned around and walked in the opposite direction. He thought he had heard something in the other room, so he went to check it out.

In the living room, a Scrabble board sat on the coffee table while the letters were spread all over the floor. She couldn't have played all alone, the officer reasoned. He noticed two tile racks sitting next to the board opposite of each other, further believing Loretta was spending time with someone just recently.

Who was she hanging out with? And where was everybody now?

He checked the bathroom, downstairs and upstairs. She wasn't there.

After a thorough search of the premises, they stepped outside onto the porch and circled the house as if Loretta was hiding behind a corner. A cow and chickens were resting in their respective homes, seeming to sense that something was amiss.

"Who's caring for the animals?" the detective said.

Another rhetorical question? The officer shrugged. "No idea."

It was clear Loretta wasn't home. And it didn't look good. In fact, it looked terrible for her, and the evidence stacked up against her.

Something occurred to the officer as his feet produced the sound of gravel cracking underneath. There was a Jeep sitting there yesterday, and now it was gone. He happened to look at the license plate, not thinking much about it, but now he had more ammunition for the case. He recalled the vanity license plate clearly: BADASS. Who wouldn't? They were called "vanity" for a reason.

As soon as he arrived at the police station, he'd look up the plate and see who it belonged to. This person should know a little something about their suspect. He hoped any additional information could lead to locking up Loretta.

CHAPTER 27

LORETTA WAS CLEARLY MISSING.

It had been over twenty-four hours since she got released from the police station, but Detective Bradley was concerned. Her house looked fairly abandoned, showing that nobody had been there in a while. She hadn't returned home after they released her. Whether it was out of panic or a deliberate attempt to conceal the crime, she'd escaped, most likely intending to disappear, change her identity, and cover up the murder entirely.

It was a good plan.

Detective Bradley saw it as a huge red flag and wanted to do something about it. In order to ensure safety for herself and society, it was crucial to locate Loretta soon if she had indeed killed Amy White. Who else could she harm while out there roaming the streets, hiding in strange places?

And now, she was both a suspect and a fugitive.

Even if Loretta hadn't killed Amy and was not dangerous, he didn't want to risk it. He had to find her as soon as possible.

Detective Bradley put together a canvasing team to walk around the residential houses and businesses and ask about Loretta's whereabouts. He was hoping for better results this time. Someone on his team called the local hospitals and emergency rooms to see if Loretta had crossed their path, but nothing of that nature occurred. Missing posters were made and plastered all over the town. Calls were made to police departments in the surrounding states, reporting Loretta missing. Maybe all the effort would help to locate her as soon as possible.

When the canvassing team stepped outside to do the work, the dark clouds rolled in, releasing the heavy rain. The raindrops fell down with vengeance as if signaling an apocalypse. Like it was a sign.

Detective Bradley sat in his office, listening to the rain beat down on the windows. He hated snow, but the sound of rain comforted him and offered peace. His thoughts on Loretta were persistent, and he couldn't get her image out of his mind. Her hollow eyes and her disheveled figure. If she was able to escape successfully, maybe she wasn't as crazy as everyone seemed to think?

The rain had already stopped when the canvassing team returned to the police station. Their clothes drenched in rain, they stepped into Detective Bradley's office, looking somewhat desperate.

"What have you got?" Detective Bradley was eager to find out.

"We canvassed her entire neighborhood, went to the church near her house, stopped by all the gas stations, went to a couple of bars and restaurants..."

Detective Bradley raised his brows in anticipation. Given their face expression, it looked grim.

"...and we've got nothing, Detective. No one has seen Loretta the past few days."

Detective Bradley exhaled sharply. "Go back to her place and turn the animals to the Animal Control. We don't want them to die."

"Yes, Detective."

While the animals could still be saved, finding Loretta was a different story.

Loretta had vanished without a trace. Detective Bradley could resort to one additional measure to quickly draw attention to her disappearance. Because, given how desperate the situation seemed, any little lead could help. He picked up the phone and dialed.

CHAPTER 28

LATER THAT EVENING, Sarah was typing at her desk, with Koko sleeping on the floor by her side.

According to her book outline, she had less than ten chapters to finish her current novel draft. This one was a doozy. At sixty thousand words, she should wrap the book up and come to a conclusion, but her characters were having minds of their own. They did not want to quit.

Not that she didn't enjoy writing it. She was ready to move on from this one and start a new project. So many book ideas were twirling in her head.

She stood by to get a glass of water. Koko lifted her head, following Sarah with her eyes, then went back to sleep. The kitchen was a mess. Dirty dishes were towering in the sink, fruit flies were attacking a half-eaten apple on the counter, and the stench of the old food was unbearable. When she finished the next chapter, she'd do some cleaning. She hated how writing took her away from daily chores, but she had no choice when she was challenged against a tight deadline.

When she walked past the living room, back to her desk, she stopped and did a double take at the TV.

"Is that...is that Loretta?" she whispered.

Her image was plastered across the screen, and Sarah rubbed her eyes, unsure she was seeing it correctly. It was Loretta's mugshot, most likely recently taken by the police. Loretta looked different in the photo: not the graceful beauty Sarah was used to seeing, but a worn-down version of the woman she believed to know so well.

Sarah walked to the coffee table and retrieved the remote to turn the volume up. The reporter, with a microphone in her hand, spoke directly to the camera:

Breaking news: In a startling turn of events, the prime suspect in a high-profile murder case, Loretta Davis, has vanished without a trace, sending shockwaves through the community and intensifying the hunt for justice. Authorities are scrambling to locate the individual, whose disappearance has left investigators grappling with a potential setback in their pursuit of truth and closure for the victim's family. The suspect, who had been under close surveillance, evaded authorities, prompting widespread concern and speculation about her whereabouts and motives. As law enforcement agencies mobilize search teams and deploy resources to track down the elusive suspect, residents are urged to remain vigilant and report any sightings or relevant information that could aid in her apprehension. Stay tuned as this developing story unfolds, and the search for answers continues.

She raised her hands to her mouth, unable to get words out. What the hell was going on? Why was her friend being reported as a fugitive? A prime suspect in a murder case?

She then remembered her recent visit and the man she'd found in Loretta's house. The entire scene seemed weird. The man that left the house, enraged. Sarah had been scared he was going to hurt her, but, fortunately, he'd only seemed intent on running away from the house and never looking back.

Could the man be involved?

Was Loretta the mastermind behind the murder? The man's captivity? Sarah shook her head in disbelief.

None of this made any sense. Loretta would kill no one, as eccentric as she was sometimes. And she would never run away. Sarah didn't think she was capable of either.

Just the thought of her friend being capable of doing all these vile things made her dizzy. Sarah sat on the couch to compose herself and stared at a commercial for life insurance on the TV.

Koko woke up and came for a pat, as if sensing something could be wrong. Sarah put her hand on Koko automatically and rubbed her below her ear, her favorite spot.

"Koko, what the hell is happening?" Sarah whimpered.

Koko cocked her head to the side, her tail wagging

against the floor. The dog looked at Sarah in the eye, as if she were just about to answer her question.

Sarah sat in the same spot, mesmerized, trying to process the news. Loretta? A murderer? Jesus Christ. How was that even possible? Loretta had never killed a fly when they were hanging out as kids. But what the hell did she know? As a news and crime junkie, she'd learned everything in life was possible.

CHAPTER 29

OFFICER RUSSELL WAS IMPRESSED with Detective Bradley. He wasn't messing around.

He'd called the local news station to broadcast the missing fugitive. He'd called state troopers to make sure Loretta got caught if she crossed the border and fled Massachusetts. He'd even put a canvassing team together to expand their research. All the works.

But the fact that none of it had produced any fruitful leads led both of them to be creative. What else could they do to find her?

"Does she have any family?" the detective probed Officer Russell.

"I've searched the database, and it looks like she might have a couple of cousins on her mother's side."

"Yeah? Where do they live?"

"One is in Minnesota, and one in Texas."

"Get in touch with them and see if they might have heard from Loretta."

Officer Russell nodded and retreated to his own corner. He came inside his office, sat down, and placed his head on the chair, closing his eyes. He wanted to scream but didn't think it was efficient or appropriate. Things didn't seem to go as smoothly as he'd hoped. The search for Loretta yielded no results.

He pulled the phone numbers from the database and dialed both cousins. The first cousin, Bratt, didn't even know who the officer was talking about until he explained their lineage.

"Sorry, but I didn't even know I had a cousin named Loretta."

Officer Russell thought about what to say next and finally mustered, "Loretta Davis. She's your first cousin. Your father and her mother are siblings."

"Oh," he said in a deep voice. "Well, I don't think I ever met my aunt. She died when I was young, and we already lived in Texas. We didn't go to Massachusetts that often, even though my father was born there, you know. But maybe someday, I will. I'd like to meet this cousin of mine. What was her name again? Lynn? Lindsey?"

Officer Russell rolled his eyes, no longer interested in what Bratt had to say. "Loretta."

"Yeah. Loretta." He laughed. "I'm bad with names, you know."

He thanked the cousin, who obviously couldn't help, and dialed the other one.

Danielle knew of Loretta, but, gosh, the last time they saw each other was when they were children.

"Oh yeah. Loretta," she said. "How's she doing?"

The officer moved the phone away from his ear and looked at it with his furrowed brows. Did she think they were all long-lost buddies?

"Unfortunately, Loretta is considered the prime suspect in a murder case here in Athol, Massachusetts." Silence and a gasp travelled from the other side of the line. "She's gone missing, and the authorities are looking for her. Have you heard from her at all?"

"Oh, gosh. No." Silence. "My little cousin, Loretta, is a murderer?" Her voice pitched a few notes higher.

"Yes."

"Holy crap."

It wasn't funny, but Officer Russell smiled at the cousin's reaction. She sure was shocked. Like everyone else.

"If you hear from her at all, please call."

"Yeah, will do."

But the Officer had a feeling he'd never hear from them again. He stood up to look for the detective and report his conversations. He still had another source to investigate.

Detective Bradley was nowhere to be found. He asked the other cops, but they appeared busy, shaking their head.

The officer peeked into the conference room, but it was empty. Detective Bradley liked to spend time in this room, whether he was eating lunch or playing on his laptop, as the room was quiet. In the kitchenette, Marybelle was brewing fresh coffee, ignoring everyone in her proximity.

"Hey, have you seen Bradley?" the officer said.

"No," she said without looking at him.

Marybelle opened the dishwasher and moved the clean mugs to the cabinet shelves. Her movements were quick yet graceful. The officer was intrigued and wanted to uncover more about her. The silent and shy ones, in his experience, could be a wild ride, and when unhinged, they could be so much fun. Besides, when she was standing, she didn't look that plump. Well, somewhat, but she was still attractive and could lose weight if she worked hard at it. They didn't need to get serious or anything, but spending time with other people would certainly abate his loneliness. Make him feel more normal. A beer or two could be non-committal. And if he got lucky, well...

"Hey, Marybelle, I have a question for you."

She turned her head. "What is it?"

Her voice was raspy, as if she'd smoked all her life. And maybe she had. The police station had banned smoking around the building a few years ago, so she'd have to go far away and hide.

"I'm wondering... I'm wondering if you want to grab a beer sometime."

She turned around and looked at the officer with wide, scared eyes. A lump appeared at her throat, and she clutched the edge of the counter.

"I..." Her face flushed crimson, and she stuttered, "I'd love to, but—"

"Russell!" The detective stood behind them. "I hear you're looking for me."

"Yeah." He walked toward the detective, leaving the flustered Marybelle behind.

The detective gazed at her and as they moved enough away. "What was that all about?"

The officer shook his head. "Oh, you know. Women."

But he knew Marybelle was about to reject him, and he hated the thought. The bitch wasn't worth his time, anyway.

They walked inside the officer's office and sat down.

"Did you call?"

"Yes. No leads. They didn't hear from her."

"Nothing?" Detective Bradley bored his eyes into the officer.

"Nothing."

But the officer had another trick under his sleeve. "I think I have another connection to the suspect. Let me dig up some info, and I'll get back to you."

CHAPTER 30

THE JEEP with the BADASS vanity license plate belonged to Ethan Harrison.

Born in Cleveland, Ohio, on July 15, 1985. Had lived in Massachusetts for over ten years. Never married. His parents were still married and lived in Ohio. No siblings.

He had some questionable history of domestic abuse. Records showed his two previous partners, or girlfriends, or whatever they were, had called the cops to report him. Assault and battery. Never got arrested but had a restraining order.

Besides issues with anger management, his profile wasn't that eye-catching. Aside from the fact he sucked at his intimate relationships, he was living an otherwise ordinary life, working in IT jobs, having a good income. Graduated from the Ohio State University with good grades. Owned a single-family house in Townsend, half an hour ride from Athol.

As the officer poured over the records, his forehead

creased, and his brows furrowed. As far as he could tell, there was no familial connection between him and Loretta. But he would find out soon.

He jumped out of his seat to find the detective. He was sitting in the conference room, all alone, stuffing his mouth with a Subway sandwich.

"Hey, I think we might have another lead."

"What is it?" He spoke with his mouth full of food.

"Loretta had a guest a couple of days before her disappearance. He might know where she is. Coming?"

"Sure." He wiped his mouth and stood up, chugging his water from a bottle all at once.

What a piggish display of a man, the officer thought. But it made the detective more human, tangible; helping the officer feel less intimidated, more in charge. He needed all the confidence he could muster.

On their way to Townsend, they didn't exchange too many words. The radio broke the silence occasionally, but they both kept their thoughts to themselves.

Ethan's house was in the middle of a cul-de-sac with kick-ass curb appeal. Overgrown bushes of various colors adorned his front yard. Daisies, lilies, and heleniums decorated the house's edge, creating a pleasurable sight. The house featured solar panels on the roof. Ethan's concern for the environment further revealed his character. Maybe he wasn't as bad as his records showed?

The front porch was large, with a round table in the middle and several chairs spread around it. In the other corner was a hammock where the officer pictured Ethan resting in this quiet neighborhood. He seemed capable of taking care of his house, but not his romantic relationships.

Douche.

Envy oozed out of the officer as he thought of his shitty rental in Athol. If he ever got that promotion, he'd work on buying a single-family house, fulfilling his lifelong dream.

But it seemed Ethan didn't have trouble buying and maintaining his home. The officer already hated this guy's guts.

They pushed the doorbell and waited for the door to open. The detective checked his watch and saw it was almost two in the afternoon. Ethan may not be at home. Just as he reached for the doorbell again, the door swung wide open.

On the other side of the door stood a tall, handsome man, and the officer scanned him quickly. Ethan wore pajama bottoms and a white T-shirt; his biceps bulging through the sleeves. He had a macho-man look every man would be jealous of.

Ethan's eyes widened at the sight of two men in uniform on his porch. "Can I help you?"

"Hi, I'm Detective Bradley, and this is Officer Russell. Are you Ethan Harrison?"

"Yeah. What's this about?" He glanced in both directions up the street.

"We're here to ask you a couple of questions about Loretta Davis. Do you know her?"

Ethan snapped his head back. He scratched his head

and scanned the distance, as though he expected someone to emerge from behind the corner. "Yeah, I know her."

"Loretta Davis is missing, and she's considered the prime suspect in the murder case of Amy White. We've been looking for her everywhere with no leads whatsoever."

Silence. Ethan's eyes widened further, his mouth agape.

"Wow." He stared at Detective Bradley while running his hand through his hair. "Didn't see that coming."

"You didn't see what coming, sir?"

He shook his head. "The murder." Pause. "Yeah, but now that you're saying it, I can sort of see it."

Ethan gazed down at the floor, looking perturbed by the news.

"What do you mean by 'you can sort of see it'?" the detective probed further.

Ethan creased his forehead, as if regretting saying it. "Never mind." He lifted his hand and shook his head.

"What was the last time you saw her?"

Ethan rolled his eyes as if thinking.

"I don't know. Maybe three or four days ago."

"Not since?"

"No." Ethan looked the detective straight in the eye. Not a blink.

"What's your connection to her?"

Ethan let go of the door and stood straighter. "We dated for a few months. Nothing serious."

"How did you two meet?" the officer asked, and the detective turned to him, raising an eyebrow.

"We met online." Ethan scoffed. "If I'd known she was batshit, I never would have agreed to go out with her in the first place."

Well, both the detective and the Officer knew Loretta's history of being locked up in a loony bin. No need to question Ethan about that.

"Tell us what happened the last time you saw her? Did she say anything about leaving town?"

Ethan looked to his left, thinking, then turned back to the detective. "Nope." He shook his head slowly. "Said nothing to me."

"Did she get in touch with you the past few days?"

Ethan pressed his lips and shook his head. "Nope."

"Any idea where she could be?"

"I have no clue, officers." Ethan grabbed the door and pushed it closed slightly, looking behind his shoulder. "Any more questions? I'm working now and have a meeting in a few."

The detective nodded once. "No, that's all. If you hear from her, please call immediately."

"Okay, sure."

The detective handed him his business card, and Ethan took it and waved it before he closed the door.

"Well, that was no help," the detective said as they settled in the car.

The officer stared in front of him and watched Ethan's house and its display of perfection. Something was amiss.

He had a feeling Ethan was hiding something, that he didn't tell a complete story.

The officer clenched his hands into a fist and wanted to break the window. But he composed himself. He had to behave well in front of the detective.

CHAPTER 31

ANGER HAD RADIATED FROM LIZ, filling every inch of the bakery until Bob was choking on it. He couldn't take it anymore.

The minute Liz learned Loretta was reported missing, she'd called her friend to ask if her daughter Emma was still interested in the job.

The morning Emma arrived, Bob excused himself for the day. He didn't tell Liz where he was going or what he was going to do that day. He'd had enough of his wife.

It was an early Wednesday, and the day was perfect for a walk around the woods. He parked nearby at a place where trail maps were displayed. Since it was a weekday, he didn't think he'd run into anybody. He got out of the car and walked around to retrieve the backpack sitting on the passenger seat. Inside, he tucked in a couple of bottles of vodka, a bag of pretzels, and bottled water.

Their cabin sat about a mile from the parking lot, a good hike on a marked trail. Liz and Bob had had this cabin for God knew how long, and they'd bought it when it was dirt cheap. When times looked desperate, Liz insisted they sell it—surely, they'd make a huge profit—but Bob would rather die than let that happen. Besides, it was his only sanctuary, the place he could hide, sit by the lake, and contemplate life.

Think about all the life choices he had made—good and bad.

Sometimes he wondered if marrying Liz was a terrible choice. Before they got married, she was an absolute gem. She kept cool at the most stressful times and continued to be his rock over the years. But when the kids came, their marriage flipped, filled with unfulfilled expectations and demands. What did Liz think Bob was?

Besides, Liz didn't look as hot anymore. Gosh, when they first met, she was a total knockout. Her curves were perfect and all in the right places. The curves were now enveloped in an extra shimmer, lending a plumpness to her face. Most women could sport a short haircut, but not Liz. She looked awful.

It wasn't so much the looks that bothered Bob. He could tolerate them. It was all the other shit.

Lately, they'd been fighting about virtually everything: from bakery-related matters of household issues, to who was going to pick up dinner at the local pizza parlor. During those fights, Liz would turn into a menacing creature, her face contorted into an ugly, unrecognizable person. This was not the same woman Bob had married thirty years ago. What the fuck happened to her?

The truth was, he dreaded the current state of his marriage. He despised it, in fact. Liz's actions made him feel uneasy, and her snide comments and constant stress pushed him over the edge. She'd never learned how to be graceful. Kind. And she should really ease up on that wine.

Almost every night she came home, she'd open a bottle and go to town with it. Her lips and teeth were stained crimson, like a vampire feasting on blood. Despite Bob's warnings that her drinking had become excessive and out of control, and could cause a slew of other problems, she paid him no attention.

And that was the crux of the issue for Bob: his wife paid him no attention.

From the outside, the cabin looked like a tiny shed about to be bulldozed. Despite its grim looks, Bob could recall many happy memories there. He used to invite his buddies over for a card game and they'd pull an all-nighter, drinking and listening to music in the background. Shit, that was almost five years ago. His buddies weren't good at keeping in touch. Come to think of it, it was always Bob who initiated get-togethers at his cabin. But none of his buddies ever invited him to their place.

Bob entered the cabin, and the musty smell splashed his nostrils immediately. Once upon a time, the musty smell could be managed and kept to a minimum when he visited more often and opened all the windows to let some fresh forest air in. But age would do damage to anything. The carpet was worn out and thick with mud, dust, and dirt. The kitchenette was barely functional, but the fridge was still working, and there was running water in the sink. No hot water, though.

But still—the cabin was his, and he loved the peace that it brought him.

He sat on the couch to contemplate his next move. What would he do for the next hour? What should he do with his life? Should he consider divorcing his bitter and estranged wife? Gosh, he couldn't do that. He couldn't just uproot his life because Liz had been acting like a kid with a tantrum. What would their grown-up children say if he moved on, forgot about everything he worked so hard for all his life?

He pulled a bottle of vodka from his backpack and ran to the kitchen cabinet to retrieve an empty glass. He poured himself a healthy dose and chugged it down. It felt so good and warm. The rush of alcohol hit his brain, and he shook his head to get rid of the feeling.

In the cabin's corner was a small room, barely big enough to fit a queen-sized bed. Bob had used it as a storage space. He kneeled and lifted the secret log on the floor, revealing a Glock he'd bought many years ago. It was still there. Of course it was. There was no way anyone could stumble on it. He felt the Glock under his fingers and studied it carefully, flipping it in his hands over and over. It was fully loaded, as if waiting to be used any moment. He felt the smoothness of the plastic. His brows furrowed when he thought of all the things he could do with the gun, but luckily, he could control himself.

One bullet, and his problems could be gone.

There were so many times in the past couple of years he'd get drunk, took the Glock, put it on his temple, and wanted to pull the trigger. His quick death could solve all his problems. The issues with his finances, his wife, his love problems...all of that would be gone in an instant.

But life had ups and downs. It had promises we could never think of during desperate times. Humans were not meant to dispose of their own lives, but to run their natural course. Unless murders and wars happened. Unless a natural disaster or disease took its toll.

Besides, Bob had no guts to pull the trigger. He was a little too much in love.

Sometimes, life threw surprises at you when least expected. Who we end up loving, whose heart and soul we desire, isn't always up to us.

Bob faced the same dilemma. He'd never expected to be attracted to a woman other than his wife. He'd never suspected another woman would occupy his mind constantly, driving him crazy. And he never could have guessed that someday, the woman of his heart's choosing would be a fugitive, hiding from the world.

Loretta. He was ashamed to admit it.

He felt so betrayed.

CHAPTER 32

THAT EVENING, when he came home after questioning Ethan, Officer Russell was cranky.

He slammed the front door of his shitty apartment, causing the building to shake. Everything negative in his life crossed his mind at once. That he lived in this dingy place, that he made peanuts, and his dreams were far-fetched, that his best buddy had no time for him, that he was single with no dating prospects, that even Marybelle, that fat bitch, rejected him for a date earlier today.

Fuck this life. Things couldn't be worse.

He'd had a rough day, and he was looking forward to finishing it in front of the TV, watching a mindless movie. His stomach growled, so he went to the fridge to see what food he had inside. His eyes scanned the shelves, finding nothing, so he slammed the fridge door and cussed under his breath.

He was tired of living alone and eating frozen food and leftovers. It was on a day like this he wished he had a woman by his side who'd cook him a meal after a long day at work.

He opened the freezer and zeroed in on a frozen pizza from Trader Joe's. A four-cheese one. It wasn't his favorite, but that would be his dinner tonight. He would down it with a beer or two, savoring the simple pleasure of a quick meal after a long day. He reached for a bottle from the fridge, the condensation cool against his fingertips. As he popped the cap off, the familiar hiss of carbonation escaping brought a sense of relief. It was his moment of respite, a chance to unwind and momentarily forget the stresses of the day. With each sip, the flavors danced on his palate, and he allowed himself to sink into the comfort of the evening, the worries of the outside world fading away with each bite and sip.

After he ate, he sat on the couch and turned on Netflix to find a movie, but thoughts swirling in his head kept him unsettled. There was no way he could concentrate and sit in one place to watch a movie for more than an hour.

He grabbed the open beer bottle and headed to a small desk in the corner of his living room, where his laptop sat. An old Mac he hadn't used in ages, mainly because he had no reason to. Back in the day, when he was younger, and when emailing people was a thing, he'd spend hours catching up with friends, writing long emails to his college buddies, sending jokes in group emails, but the trend had somehow died. People were only texting nowadays, and that had dwindled over time as well.

He took a swig of his beer and opened the laptop. In

the browser, he typed in *Date Dazzle*, a dating site he'd signed up many years ago. He glanced at the ceiling to recall his password, which he knew by heart since he only used a handful of passwords that he rotated.

Foreveryours95

As soon as he logged on, he'd noticed the notifications. A smile formed on his face, but it disappeared as soon as he realized these messages were from *Date Dazzle*, asking if he wanted to renew his subscription. As he went through old emails from women he tried to date, he realized he was the one who'd ghosted them.

Shit. No wonder he felt so lonely. He'd never given these women a chance.

His profile was outdated. The main profile picture was taken over five years ago, and he'd looked much thinner and happier. He remembered exactly when that picture was taken. He was out on a hike in the White Mountains with a date on a sunny June day. His date snapped that photo of him. Whatever happened to Emily? She was a fun date, but as soon as she'd learned he was a cop, her face grew sullen, and he'd never heard from her again after that. But he might try his luck again.

He went into the search box and filtered women's age from twenty-five to thirty-five. Location, within ten miles.

"Wow."

The glare of the computer brightened his face, etched in surprise. There were so many results coming up. It was unnerving to know there were so many single women in his proximity. Yet, it kept him hopeful that maybe one of them would catch his eye.

He scrolled down, checking out the faces of the women on the page. They looked pretty and smiley and ready to mingle. But none of them stood out. Except one. He leaned forward and squinted, making sure he was seeing right.

It was her. Loretta. The fugitive.

He clicked on her profile and stared back at her big blue eyes. Her profile photo looked like it came right out of a magazine. Nothing close to the mugshot in the police database. He cocked his head and looked at her, mesmerized, admiring her facial features. There was only a small amount of makeup on her eyes, and some lipstick. She didn't need much in terms of beautifying herself. She was already beautiful enough.

Checking into her dating profile could help glean more information about her. It could help connect the dots.

Under her interests, she'd put down board games, collecting dolls, live music, watching reality shows, spending time in the nature. Her profile seemed rather sparse with information. That was probably okay with most men who might have stumbled upon her profile. Her exuding beauty was enticing enough. But there was not much information to advance their search. In fact, her profile was quite boring.

As he scrolled up to the top, something caught his eye.

He noticed Loretta checked off her profile status under "In a relationship," but she seemed to have appeared online only five days ago. That seemed strange to Will. If she was in a relationship, wouldn't she delete her profile and not look back? Was Ethan her guy?

Obviously, because he'd said so earlier. They couldn't be that happy together if she kept re-logging on *Date Dazzle*. Maybe Ethan was a bigger loser than he thought. His fancy house and good looks all could be a big fat lie.

He turned on the printer and enlarged Loretta's profile photo. Adjusting his chair and sipping his beer, he waited until the printer spit out Loretta's image. It was an old, slow printer, but it functioned.

At the last leg, he grabbed the sheet of paper and pulled it out of the printer, almost ripping it at the edge. He set the beer bottle on the desk and hurried to a room next to the bathroom, shaking the photo in the air.

CHAPTER 33

FINDING LORETTA WAS PROVING to be fruitless.

She could be anywhere, really. The world was so vast. Detective Bradley had seen people disappear, change their identity, transform their looks, you-name-it.

Several murder cases in his lifetime remained unre-solved, either because concrete evidence didn't exist, or the murderer could get away. It wasn't the ideal outcome, but at some point, you have to surrender and walk away.

He was toying with the idea of reaching out to the FBI, but he thought better of it. Last time he did it, it took them forever to even respond.

This whole missing situation bothered Detective Bradly. Was it possible that not one person came forward to report seeing her? Could she be this crafty to mask her disappearance and not leave a trace?

Maybe he should call the FBI and request their help in case Loretta crossed the state border and found refuge elsewhere.

He dug deeper and found that she'd not used her credit card for more than a few days. It could be a clever way of disguising her whereabouts, and she could be living on cash. But for how long could she sustain that kind of living? It would take lots of cash to do that.

Something didn't seem right to Detective Bradley. They'd interviewed her neighbors, friends, the bakery owners, her boyfriend, and not one person had any idea where she could be. Not to mention none of them even cared. How could she fall off the face of the Earth?

He walked to the front desk and found Marybelle sitting at her desk and staring at the computer. She creased her forehead as if she was deep in thought.

"Hey, Marybelle."

She gasped, jumped in her chair and turned around to face the detective. All the blood had drained from her face as she kept staring at him.

"Sorry, I didn't mean to scare you."

"Oh," she said. "That's okay. I didn't see you coming."

"Hey, have you seen Officer Russell?"

She swallowed a lump in her throat and looked away, her head shaking fast. "No. No, I haven't."

Detective Bradley scoffed, feeling peeved. The guy was always missing when he had to talk to him.

"Can you tell him to see me when he swings by?"

"I will."

He turned around and thought about Marybelle's strange reaction at the mention of Russell's name. Did she have a crush on him? It was possible. Russell was a stud, and he could have any woman. Which made him wonder how this guy could be single. When he was his age, girls were all over him, and vice versa, until he met his current wife.

But he got it, because there was something about Officer Russell he couldn't quite define. Being a loner could do that to a person. Your social compass could get compromised during deep solitude.

Detective Bradley returned to his desk, the weight of Loretta's fugitive status heavy on his mind. He scrolled through his notes, scrutinizing every detail of the case once again. There had to be something he was overlooking, some clue that would lead him to her. Bradley scanned through the report, his heart sinking as he realized there were no significant leads.

He couldn't allow Loretta to slip through his fingers, becoming just another unresolved case haunting the department. Or the town.

How about social media? Did Russell go through her profiles on Facebook or Instagram? He opened his computer and typed Facebook into the browser. Loretta Davis. His search yielded many results of the namesake across the country. It was a popular name.

One that said "from Athol" drew his attention. It had to be her, because, according to their database, there was only one Loretta Davis living in Athol. He clicked on it. The profile was quite bare, and the profile picture was a creepy doll. He could still see her friends. He didn't find the list impressive. All fifty-three of them. She either wasn't popular or active on social media.

He clicked on the friends' list and searched for any names that could tie her to Amy White. Was she friends with Amy White? If she truly believed Amy was responsible for delivering her stillborn child, that would have been her motive to kill her, and chances were slim they were friends.

How about any other names that had come up during the investigation? Liz? Bob? Well, it looked like Bob was a friend, but he'd been cleared as a suspect in Amy's murder and knew nothing about Loretta's disappearance.

Exasperated, Detective Bradley sank into the chair and let out a sigh. He squinted and looked at the screen, seeing a familiar name on the friends' list. He leaned forward to better look.

Then his eyes bulged.

Was there a deeper connection with this unexpected name that he'd overlooked? Lost in thought, he couldn't shake the conviction that he'd made a major discovery.

CHAPTER 34

THE DARKNESS VEILED THE CABIN, making Loretta nervous that she could see nothing, not even a finger in front of her.

The moon had to be hidden behind thick clouds, disallowing any light to project into the forest. She curled up in the bed, rubbing her skin, which was covered in goosebumps from the cold. Chill was more common at nights as the summer slipped away. She would die for a blanket just about now.

The only way to handle the thirst, the hunger, the cold was to numb her brain, force herself to have an out-of-body experience. She quieted her mind and counted to a hundred. When she got to the number, she started all over again. Time might pass quicker if she focused on something, anything, rather than the condition she was in or who her captor was.

Couldn't even guess.

And frankly, it didn't matter who or why.

The cold prevented her from falling asleep for hours, but eventually she did. Before that, her life flashed in front of her as if she were on a deathbed, about to say farewell to the sad life she had had.

As she sailed into dreamland, her mother appeared out of nowhere, wearing a white dress, smiling at Loretta. Like Loretta, she was beautiful. Her mother extended her arms and smiled at her daughter, inviting her to a warm hug. As Loretta reached for her, her mother fell into the abyss, still smiling.

In the subconscious of a dream, she heard her father sing a lullaby. Her favorite was *You are My Sunshine,* and his voice stuck in her mind forever.

The cabin seemed to exhale with the shifting of the night, its creaks and groans joining the nocturnal symphony of the forest. Loretta's dreams twirled at the periphery of her mind, a jumbled mix of recollections and worries. She drifted in and out of sleep, the boundary between reality and illusion blurring with each passing moment.

In her dream, she aimlessly explored the hallways of her childhood residence, the walls reverberating with murmured secrets and abandoned vows. Shadows danced in the corners of her vision, elusive and ephemeral, like ghosts from a past she couldn't escape.

She reached out, fingers brushing against the cool surface of the walls, searching for something she couldn't name. Her mother's laughter echoed in her ears, a haunting melody that tugged at her heartstrings with bittersweet nostalgia.

But as she turned the corner, the familiar hallway stretched endlessly before her, the walls closing in like the jaws of some unseen predator. Panic clawed at her throat, threatening to choke her with its icy grip.

Then, just as suddenly as it had begun, the dream shifted, morphing into a hazy montage of faces and places long forgotten. She saw herself as a child, laughing and playing in the sunlight, oblivious to the darkness that lurked just beyond the horizon.

But even in her dreams, reality intruded like a sharp thorn, piercing the fragile veil of illusion. Images flashed before her eyes: the twisted wreckage of a car, the wail of sirens in the night, the hollow emptiness of a home torn apart by tragedy.

And through it all, her father's voice sang softly in the background, a beacon of light in the suffocating darkness. *You are My Sunshine*, he crooned, his words a soothing balm for her fractured soul.

The dream was unraveling, slipping through her fingers like grains of sand. She reached out, desperate to hold on to the fragments of her past, but they slipped from her grasp, leaving her alone in the stiff embrace of the night.

When she finally awoke, the first rays of dawn were filtering through the cracks in the cabin walls, painting the room in a soft, golden light. Loretta blinked, disoriented and weary, as the memories of the night before flooded back to her in a rush of confusion and fear.

She sat up slowly, rubbing the sleep from her eyes as she took in her surroundings. Silence bathed the cabin, the only sound being the gentle rustle of leaves outside the window.

With a heavy sigh, Loretta swung her legs over the edge of the bed. Her body ached with stiffness from sleeping on the hard mattress, but she pushed through the discomfort, determined to face whatever lay ahead.

Despite the fear and uncertainty that gnawed at her insides, Loretta refused to surrender to despair. She'd find a way out of this nightmare, she vowed, no matter the cost.

CHAPTER 35

HER GROGGINESS from sleep persisted throughout the day.

The dreams of her mother stuck in her mind, and she felt haunted by her absence all these years. Her father's lullaby came as a welcome gift as she tried to survive this terrible nightmare. Suddenly, they became the reason to survive. They gave her strength to keep going, even when every step felt like wading through molasses.

Memories of her parents, their love, their sacrifices, now fueled her resolve. She clung to their whispered encouragements like a lifeline in the stormy sea of her life. With each passing moment, their spirits walked beside her, guiding her through the darkest corners of despair. In memory of them, she promised to persevere and transcend the difficulties that could overpower her.

They were her beacons of hope in the endless days and nights.

In terms of her physical condition, Loretta felt as though she was still a weak child learning to crawl.

Hunger and thirst became stronger and deeper overnight. She lifted her head, but it fell back to the bed involuntarily. Strength had left her, and she could barely move. The shackles around her ankle anchored her to the same spot, so even if she wanted to move, she couldn't.

What had prompted her captor to lock her up in this terrible place? Who was he? What did he want from her? Outside, the birds beckoned with their song and screeches, but there was no way out. She turned around slowly, pain throbbing through her body. She whimpered as her bones hit against the uncomfortable bed.

She stared at the ceiling, reciting prayers she'd memorized as a child. Throughout her adolescence, Father Lee had guided her through many life challenges, so she imagined what he'd say if he were here now. Many times, he'd tell her to keep it cool. That the mind could make things much darker, so it was important to keep her head screwed on right. And to pray. Believe in whatever was out there that kept us safe and alive.

Whenever she experienced a high level of distress, she recounted random facts in her head to allow for time to pass by. Her thoughts were filled with facts from school and from the news or TV.

The longest river in Europe is Volga. It flows through eleven major cities. None of which Loretta ever visited.

The highest mountain in the world is Mount Everest.

In high school, she remembered learning how tall the mountain was. 8,848 meters. It was easy to remember because it had too many eights. It translated to 29,031 feet.

If Loretta was ever on *Jeopardy*, she wondered how she'd fare. Her head was full of useless facts, and that seemed to be the most important thing on the show. Sprinkled with self-confidence and some strategy, of course. How you wagered if you got a double jeopardy was important. And then, the speed. If you clicked on that button fast enough, you were ahead of your opponents. Gosh, she'd love to be on the show someday.

If she ever survived this horror.

Today, 230 million women around the world have their genitals cut because of their country's tradition.

230 million. Loretta read this in the news recently and cringed at the thought.

This would never appear on *Jeopardy*, but it was engrained in her mind. She couldn't shake it off as she imagined the pain and suffering these girls went through.

The six most common elements in living things are carbon, hydrogen, oxygen, nitrogen, phosphorus, and sulfur. Atoms of these elements combine and form thousands of large molecules. These large molecules make up the structures of cells and carry out many processes essential to life.

Now, that was a thought. Life. A strange yet beautiful concept. So many galaxies in the universe, and we were given a life in the Milky Way. Did other celestial entities exist elsewhere? Who knew? Either way, if they existed or not, human life was just as fascinating.

Oftentimes, Loretta thought about why some lives were given and others taken. Why did her mother depart the world so suddenly? Her physical presence would never be restored to the earth. But Loretta knew her mother was still here in spirit.

She could sometimes hear voices whisper in her ear, and she was certain it was her mother talking to her. Giving her advice. Not that she remembered her mother's voice, but her father often described her as an angel. Every time he talked about her, he'd look out in a distance and his eyes would well up.

It had been no surprise he'd never remarried. As far as Loretta could tell, he never even dated another woman.

Loretta was his world.

The square root of 169 is thirteen.

Thirteen was Loretta's favorite number. Thirteen was the age through which she'd cruised in innocence and happiness. Her father was good and devoted to her, and he provided her with all the means of being a normal teenager. Since she was an only child and had lost her mother at a young age, he'd cherished her like the most valuable thing in the world.

When she turned fourteen, her life turned for the worse and it stayed that way. Her mind suddenly flipped a switch, and she changed overnight. She felt demons possessed her body, but she couldn't control them.

At school, math wasn't her cup of tea, but she'd picked it up quickly. She always got good grades on the exams.

And then, everything declined, including her grades. She sprouted into a beautiful young woman, curves all in the right places. Boys her age were dying to be in her presence. However, because she was too shy, people interpreted her demeanor as arrogance, so she suffered the consequences.

In the school's hallway, her classmates would constantly poke and probe her, laugh at her, call her "Crazy Loretta." Sure, she had an occasional fit and acted irrationally, but sometimes she felt those kids pushed her to that stage.

Sometimes beauty could bring ugliness into the world. Beauty could be a liability, not an asset.

Like in Loretta's case.

Well, too bad. There was nothing she could do about her looks.

Her mind wandered as she lay on the bed helplessly. Despite her distracted state, moments of hunger or thirst brought her back to reality.

Hours passed, and at dusk, Loretta heard a noise outside her door. Was she dreaming? She lifted her head to check the commotion. Fear trickled down her spine, as she didn't know who or what she was about to face.

The lock rumbled on the other side of the door. She heard her captor spit out swear words.

She recognized his voice immediately.

Her blood froze.

She imagined his face etched in anger, like she'd seen many times before. It was a matter of time before he opened the door. Within seconds, she'd have to face him again, reluctantly, but she had no choice.

She was as good as dead. He was here to make her pay her dues.

She curled up in bed and cried. The door opened with full force, but she couldn't make herself turn to see him. A knot tightened in her belly.

An instant later, she felt his presence hovering over her, a shadow of menace covering her fragile frame. His cologne, strangely familiar, replaced the scent of musty air. The crumpling sound amplified her fear until he revealed it was just a bag of food he'd brought.

"Here. I brought you some pastries," he said. "Get up!"

She struggled to turn around, seeing the pastry enticingly displayed on his black leather glove.

Why was he wearing gloves? Loretta didn't have the answer. Not that she cared now. He'd brought her food.

The smell of warm pastry wafted through the air, making Loretta hungrier. She turned back around, avoiding her captor's eyes, and grabbed the food out of his hands, placing it in her mouth like a wild animal. She'd barely chewed it up before she bit into it again.

The captor walked out of the room, then back in, carrying a gallon of water in his hands. Loretta bulged her eyes at it and stopped chewing, attempting to reconcile what she was seeing. He handed it to her, but the weight of it made her drop it on the bed.

"Clumsy." He mocked her.

He grabbed the water and helped her drink; the stream missing her mouth and dropping on her torso.

Refueled, she felt alive again, even though she was sure her death under her captor's hand was imminent.

Teenage pregnancies result in premature death. Teenagers who had babies were twice as likely to die before the age of thirty-one.

CHAPTER 36

THE DAY AFTER, the police station appeared to be in a state of uproar.

No one could believe that the chief was a sleezy bastard. Chief Blake, of all people. The kind and caring guy who'd stop and inquiry the janitor about his family. The guy who used to swear by his career, because he really seemed to care for people. The guy who used to bring donuts for the entire station every Friday morning.

And look at him now. A fucking bastard and a pervert.

His colleagues were in utter shock. The younger ones, who admired him, appeared troubled and struggled to understand how those closest to them could be so deceitful.

Officer Russell had walked into the station, only to find an aura of grief in the air. Everyone walked by him, gazing down at the floor. But soon, he found out why.

While Chief Blake was out for his family emergency, a young officer had walked into his office and accidentally discovered porn videos of people groping dead bodies. The news was so vile that it reached the town council immediately.

The chief, looking disheveled, ran his hand through his thinning hair, as he retrieved his belongings, his eyes bulging. He informed the officer that he'd been instructed to not return to the station indefinitely.

The officer couldn't help wondering. Could the chief have done it?

He was a cop.

He knew how to get away with a crime.

Officer Russell watched the chief quickly transform from a confident, strongly opinionated man to a sleazeball. "Hey." He stood above him, resting his hands on his belt, watching the sad display of the man in trouble.

The chief gazed at him and put his head down. Then he whispered, "I didn't do it."

Officer Russell nodded, but he remembered the chief's demeanor when they went to the coroner's office to examine Amy White's dead body. His cheeks had flushed in embarrassment, as if he had something to hide.

"They're still investigating," the officer said.

The chief shook his head. "I'm screwed."

The chief leaned forward and placed his head between his hands, visibly shaking as tears rolled down his face. The officer placed his hand on his shoulder. "Hey, want a cup of coffee?"

The chief nodded. "Sure, yeah." He wiped a tear from his face.

"Be right back."

The Officer rushed through the police station to the kitchenette. The coffee carafe was empty, but the coffee machine was still on, and the coffee on the ring was burning and causing a stench.

The Officer turned around, looking for Marybelle. "Where the fuck is she?" he whispered.

Another police officer, the newest recruit, Dan, entered the kitchenette.

"Where's Marybelle?" Officer Russell grunted.

"Didn't you hear?" Dan said.

"Hear what? The chief stuff?"

"No." Dan shook his head.

What? Was there more information to be heard?

"Marybelle quit yesterday."

"What? Quit? Why?"

Dan shrugged. "Beats me."

"Did she come to the station and give her notice...or?"

"Called after work and said she wasn't coming back tomorrow. Or ever." He shrugged. "Anyway, you know how this thing works?"

Dan pointed at the coffee machine.

Officer Russell stared at the police officer in disbelief. Marybelle quit? It couldn't have anything to do with him asking her out for a beer, could it?

He turned around and faced the coffee machine. "Yeah. I do. Give me a second."

While he was making coffee, shock vibrating through him, Dan continued, "Well, it's kind of weird that she quit at the same time the chief got...you know, discovered," he scoffed. "So, they are looking for her to question her about the whole thing. You know, in case it was somehow related to her notice."

The two stood by the coffee machine in silence, waiting for coffee to finish brewing. Officer Russell wanted to ask more questions, but he was at a loss for words. He didn't know what to say.

Things were getting bizarre. They weren't adding up. He hoped things would play out okay in the end.

When the coffee finished brewing, he poured two cups —one for the chief and one for him—and put two packs of sugar in one, stirring it with a stick. He said goodbye to Dan, who was now pouring his own much-needed coffee. Officer Russell walked carefully so he didn't spill the hot beverages all over himself or the floor. When he got to the corner of the office, the chair stood empty. The chief was gone. Officer Russell looked around to search for him, but all he could see was empty space.

CHAPTER 37

LORETTA HAD BEEN MISSING for three days with no clues or leads on her whereabouts.

Now that the chief had been suspended, Detective Bradley was put in charge of the investigation. Detective Bradley dismissed the incident with the chief. That was an unfortunate accident. Such a nice guy and all. But he couldn't afford to dwell on it. He had his priorities.

He was growing frustrated, because there wasn't substantive evidence Loretta was present at the murder site of Amy White. The anonymous call could be a hoax. There wasn't any physical evidence to guide them to the murderer. What he'd seen on Facebook, under the list of Loretta's friends, seemed shocking and may be potentially significant, but that wasn't the stone he wanted to turn. He had no time to waste.

If they could find Loretta, they could interrogate her to submit, but she was nowhere to be found, and it was like she'd fallen through the earth. If she confessed to the murder, they could then proceed with a trial, deciding to either send her to jail or a mental institution, depending on what was deemed more suitable, ultimately closing the case. Detective Bradley could return to his unit with a clear conscience.

Detective Bradley went as far as to speculate that someone might have taken revenge on Loretta and killed her. Her body could be lying somewhere in a ditch. It could be dismembered and destroyed, its traces never to be found.

There had been many unresolved murder cases. It was easier to get away with murder than people thought. In his years of practice, he'd seen it all. All sorts of motives.

The pettiest kinds were pathetic. It would make him sick to his stomach, and angry, when he'd discovered their motive.

He might try and go back to her house to investigate any evidence of her return. He'd seen that before, too. A murderer in hiding, but occasionally going back home for the sake of less turbulent times. Besides, it didn't seem that she'd left the state. The law enforcement in all states were on high alert, searching for the fugitive, but nothing had come up.

He stood up from the chair and walked around the police station, looking for Officer Russell. He walked past his office, noticing it empty. He lifted his hand to check the time—it was eight in the morning. He should be in the office by now. Could he have overslept? That was impossible. Officer Russell was usually here on time, eager to tackle whatever tasks were ahead.

He went to the kitchenette and ran into a young officer with red hair and freckles on his nose. "Hey, you seen Russell at all?"

The kid creased his forehead. "No."

"Did you see him at all this morning?" Bradley pressed on.

"Oh, I think he took the day off."

"Day off?"

"Yeah. Apparently, he was shaken by what happened to the chief and needed time to process it all."

The detective scoffed and shook his head. "Jesus."

"You know, these two were super chummy. So, it's not surprising."

"I guess."

Detective Bradley walked out of the police station and took off in his car, driving in a familiar direction. He passed by the bakery and almost wanted to pay it a visit, ask if Loretta might have returned, but if there was any place to visit while in hiding, it would definitely not be a workplace.

He turned to the gravel road leading to Loretta's house, noticing the eerie silence. The woods on the other side of the house looked as they held a deep, dark secret. When he parked, he sat in his car, observing the house from a close distance. He noticed nothing unusual about it. Nothing seemed to differ from the last time they came to check.

He got out of his car and walked around. Around a

hundred feet from the porch was a big hole he didn't remember seeing last time. Was it there before? His memory could be tricky sometimes; that was why he liked to bring another officer along, so he wouldn't second-guess himself.

Where the hell was Russell? *Day off, my ass.*

Annoyance washed over him. He could use Russell's younger brain to rely on.

He stood above the hole and wondered what purpose it would have served. Strange. The cow and chickens had been taken away to a safe place, so the barn appeared devoid of any life.

He walked up to the porch and placed his head against the window, cupping it with his hands. The hallway looked untouched since he last saw it. Hooks on the wall were adorned with jackets of various colors. A single side table stood in a corner, with the top drawer wide open. The small rug stood at the same angle in the middle. Beyond the hallway, on the left side, he observed the kitchen, and while squinting, he saw the same pile of dishes sitting in the sink. On their initial visit to the house, they couldn't stand the stench and the flies swarming around the dishes. He imagined it all stunk even more, and he was happy he didn't need to witness it.

There was nothing in and around the house to suggest that Loretta might have returned.

Throughout his career, he'd been thorough, and he wouldn't miss a beat. But something in his gut told him he wouldn't find anything.

Something hinted silently this might be a dead case already. A part of him wanted to give up. But giving up was not an option for Detective Bradley. Despite the sinking feeling in his gut, he knew he had to press on. Too much was at stake—the truth had to be unearthed, justice served.

CHAPTER 38

THE WATER OVERFLOWED as Loretta gulped it down, leaving her chest wet.

As she drank, she felt reborn. Her captor still hovered above her, watching her splash herself. He made a face of disgust, then moved over to the window to open it. She glanced at him, watching his strong physique lift the windowpane. Age and under-use had glued the windowpane to the frame. He grunted as he pulled it up with difficulty.

The fresh breeze enveloped the room, giving Loretta a moment of reprieve. Taking a deep breath, she closed her eyes and transported herself to another place. She missed freedom, her home, all the things associated with the nature.

Her captor's voice reeled her back in. He spotted dried feces in the room's corner and coughed in disgust.

"You filthy animal." He wrinkled his nose.

The small room didn't have a toilet. What was she supposed to do?

"I've spent all morning doing chores for you." He walked out of the room and returned with another bag in his hand. He threw it at her. "Here. Wear this."

Loretta spread opened the bag and pulled out a gray cardigan. It delighted her to see it, so she placed it on her chest and sniffed it. It smelled new. She put it on and felt the comfort of the wool.

"I stopped by the bakery, too. They've already replaced you," he scoffed.

Loretta winced. Like any workplace, it was easy to replace a worker, just as easy as putting on a new pair of socks. But it was the least of her concerns. All she wanted was to survive. Job opportunities would come.

He sat down at the edge of the bed, studying Loretta. He cocked his head and squinted his eyes. He shook his head only so slightly, obviously pondering about something. Seconds later, an uproarious laughter came out of his mouth, then he stood up and walked to the other side of the bed.

He stared down at her as he said, "You see, I'm taking care of you, Loretta. Like in good old days."

Loretta directed a downward gaze at him. The good old days were fleeting, and she could only recall their remnants. She didn't want to remember most of it. She wondered what he wanted from her now. They'd made a deal. She would never rat him out and tell anyone what had happened in their past. Because, if she did, he'd probably kill her this time.

"I met your boyfriend yesterday." He mockingly made quotation marks with his fingers in the air. "A handsome devil, for sure."

Loretta's eyes bulged at his words. By boyfriend, did he mean Ethan? And if so, how did the two meet? Who freed him from the basement? A part of her was relieved, because at least she didn't need to worry about his captivity anymore.

"Did you lock him up in the basement like you used to lock me up?"

Loretta winced at the question. She didn't need reminders while her captivity weighted heavy on her. Besides, now wasn't the time to confess her transgressions.

They stared at each other motionless.

"Where did you meet him? Was he okay?" the sound of her own voice surprised her.

Officer Russell bulged his eyes at her; his face reddened in anger.

"So, you care about him, but you never cared about me?" he retorted, then slapped Loretta hard, causing her to fall on the bed and hit her head against the wall. In a state of helplessness, her eyes shut as a tear escaped.

"After all the love I'd given you, you still treated me like shit." His disgust was palpable. "I saw you parading with him around the town like you guys own it. He seems like an arrogant son of a bitch. And you looked so smitten."

Did Will stalk her? Or did he just happen to be there at the same time?

Silence filled the room. Loretta didn't know what to make of this. It was true she and Ethan had gone out to a restaurant a few times in downtown Athol, but she didn't see anybody familiar. She was peeved to discover that Will had been watching her.

"Are you in love with him?"

Loretta sensed jealousy in his voice as he took a step closer with clenched fists. She stared at one spot, pretending she hadn't heard the question. It didn't matter what she was going to say; Will would ignite and punish her just the same.

"Did you hear me?" he screamed. "Are you in love with him, you filthy whore?"

Loretta couldn't say a word. His rage and jealousy made her uneasy, and she didn't want to provoke him and make things worse.

He left the room, giving her relief. She was confused about what was happening. And why, after so many years, was Will after her again? Didn't they already settle the old dispute?

He returned to the room with renewed energy. He had a plastic bucket, torn at the edges, in his hand. Loretta cracked her eyes and watched him move around the room. He approached the window and shut it tight, then placed the bucket in the room's corner, and turned to look at her.

"Use the bucket from now on. Okay?" He paced

around the room then stopped in his tracks to glance at her. "You'll be here for a while. You're reported missing."

Loretta remained silent, but in her head, she wondered what that meant. She knew he'd hidden her in a remote location, but where?

"They still think you're the prime suspect and that you killed Amy." Will smiled, as if he enjoyed the fact that he could orchestrate this so well and still be covert about it.

Loretta kept her eyes fixed on the figure looming before her. She gazed at the chain occasionally and looked at Will, hoping he'd take the key, unlock the chain and set her free.

"Let me go," she whispered, her voice barely above the sound of her own racing heartbeat.

"What did you say?" His voice was like ice, sending shivers down her spine.

"Let me go. You know I didn't do it." Her words trembled on the edge of desperation, pleading for mercy from a man who seemed devoid of empathy.

He laughed, a chilling sound that echoed off the walls of the room. "Oh, Loretta. You're so cute when you're desperate."

Tears welled in Loretta's eyes as she met his gaze, searching for any flicker of humanity in the depths of his stony stare. "I didn't kill Amy," she insisted.

And if that was the reason she was held hostage in this strange place, then he better let her go now, because she was innocent.

"Oh, I know." His words froze her in place as she struggled to comprehend their meaning. He scratched his head and turned around, his back to her as he stared out the window.

She watched him warily, her breath catching in her throat as she waited for his next move. His hands rested on his waist, his body swaying from side to side, a subtle movement that betrayed the tension coiled beneath his calm facade.

"I killed Amy."

His words hung in the air like a death sentence, each syllable dripping with menace and malice. Loretta's heart seized in her chest, her mind reeling as she tried to make sense of the revelation.

"But now, I'm not really sure it was the right thing to do, Loretta. And if I've made a mistake killing her, it's all your fault."

As he stepped towards the door, a wave of terror washed over her, threatening to engulf her in its icy embrace. "I'll be back tonight," he called out over his shoulder, his voice a taunting echo.

Loretta's breath caught in her throat as she watched him disappear into the shadows, his footsteps fading into a distance. Once again, she found herself alone, hugging herself tightly, filled with fear and uncertainty.

Tonight, she knew, would bring only more terror, more danger, more unanswered questions. The only remaining lifeline was hope.

CHAPTER 39

OFFICER RUSSELL—OR Will, though his mom called him Willy—had a decent childhood.

His parents only had him, and they allowed him to behave however he wished with little repercussions. He grew up confident and self-assured. And handsome. Gosh, every girl in high school would salivate at the sight of him, hoping he'd pay them attention, or eventually ask them out. They sought his presence, hovering around the places he was most likely going to be.

He knew of his aura and power, and he took advantage of it.

In junior high, he realized he wanted to become a cop. He wasn't good at school, and it didn't interest him much, but being authority would quickly elevate his status. In his mind, he already was a cop when he was in high school. In fact, the police station was located right next to it, so while listening to his teachers lecturing, he'd watch the cops going in and out with their pistols hanging on their waists. He wanted to be like them.

Like many other boys, he was interested in girls, but no one came close to making him as smitten as Loretta did.

She practically ruined him.

He wasn't particularly proud of it, and he didn't want to get his guard down. He pretended he was playing it cool around her, but the truth was, he was dying to be around her all the time. He wrote her letters when they first went on a date, and he'd done anything to keep her interested in him. Other boys in high school eyed Loretta all the time. That nerdy Tim came close, but Will snatched her up. Once he did, they became a couple that every high schooler seemed to envy.

But it backfired. Will had never suspected how complicated their relationship would become. Even to this day.

The morning he visited her in the cabin to give her food and water, he decided to skip taking the whole day off, and instead headed to the police station. It was a better alternative than staying home alone and pouting all day.

When he arrived, he was still reeling. Anger etched his face as he walked into the police station, with his hands clenched. He couldn't believe that the wretch asked about Ethan. It was difficult to accept that she cared about someone else more than him, and rejection stung. Like it did many years ago. As he walked through the police station, he didn't pay anyone attention, and didn't even notice that Marybelle had already been replaced—an older woman was sitting at the front desk, leaning forward, and adjusting her glasses as she stared at the computer. Only later, he would learn their HR found someone temporarily.

When he walked into his office, he was surprised to see Detective Bradley sitting at his desk. That pissed him off even more, but he subsided his anger by taking a deep breath.

"Hey." Bradley waved at him.

"Hey. What are you doing in my office?"

"I just got in. I thought I heard you in the back, so I waited here."

"What's up, Detective? Something I can help with?"

Will's face remained poker. He didn't want to give any sign he was agitated by visiting the fugitive this morning everyone was still looking for.

Detective Bradley shook his head, "Wanted to check if there're any more leads on the Amy White murder case. Or Loretta."

Officer Russell shook his head. "No. Nothing."

Fear shot down his spine as he imagined Bradley suspecting something was amiss. The detective stood up from Russell's chair and proceeded toward the door.

"Did you hear about the chief?" he said.

Now Russell believed he was here to gossip, or whatever else he wanted to do to kill his time, but Russell didn't have time for it.

"What about the chief?"

Bradley kept studying his face, keeping his eyes on him.

"There might be some evidence someone framed him.

They're still investigating. Plus, Marybelle had nothing to do with it, as initially thought."

Russell snapped back his head and bulged his eyes. "Wow."

"Even if they find proof, he is still not returning to his post. He has retired," Detective announced.

"That's a bit of a surprise," Russell said.

Like Officer Russell, Chief Blake lived for his career. This was why the two got along.

Bradley brushed him as he passed by, turned around, and said, "I guess it's your lucky day."

Russell stood at the door and watched Bradley disappear around the corner. Was it too late to stop him and ask what he meant? He decided against it.

He'd already had his fair share of agitation today.

CHAPTER 40

DARKNESS HAD SETTLED upon the woods when Loretta woke up from her slumber.

She shivered from the cold even though the warm cardigan was on. The food and water Will gifted her this morning gave her some strength, but not enough to keep awake and plot her escape.

She was sure he was going to kill her eventually. She had to get out of there somehow, and soon.

Outside, close to the cabin, a howl of animals called for a prey. It was probably hungry coyotes, circling around, sensing their next catch nearby. She'd seen them around her house so many times, surrounding the chicken coop, hoping to snatch one or two.

She wondered what was happening to her house at the moment. She had no one in the world to care for it, and she surely hoped the animals would survive.

That all of them would survive.

At least Ethan did. Thank goodness.

The cabin couldn't be far from her house—only a few miles. She recognized the woods by looking out the window and spotting tall pine trees common to the Bearsden Forest conservation. Though, she couldn't guess in a million years who the cabin belonged to. Someone must have permanently abandoned it, and Will had to know about it.

The sound of the front door opening echoed through the space. Like he promised, Will was back. He unlocked Loretta's room and walked in with a plastic bag in his hand.

He trudged up to the bed and dropped the bag. Loretta could see his face through the moonshine: his eyes were narrow and his jaw tight. It was dark, too dark, to see any details, but the moonshine was strong enough for Loretta to notice his menace projecting out of him.

There were no working lights in the cabin. Will probably preferred it that way.

"I brought you dinner." He smirked at her.

His face skin shone against the moonlight, revealing a fresh shave. He smelled of cologne and wore a simple T-shirt and a pair of jeans, looking different from his usual police uniform. And the gloves. If he didn't have that scary look on his face, he'd be a lot handsomer.

Loretta slowly took the bag and retrieved a piece of bread and a can of sardines. Under normal circumstances, she hated fish, and Will knew it.

She struggled to open the can, as she had no strength.

Will snatched it out of her hand and opened it for her with ease.

The sardine smell made her puke, but hunger prevailed. She chewed the food slowly but couldn't bring herself to swallow, so she threw up at the bedside.

Will put his knuckle to his mouth. "God damn it, Loretta."

She wiped her mouth with the back of her hand and gazed at Will, noticing the disgust on his face.

"You look like a hot mess," he said. She gazed down, avoiding his eyes, feeling ashamed. "If you're good, I'll let you take a shower one of these days."

She assumed there was more to the cabin beyond this room, and the bathroom had to be on the other side of the wall. Would he free her from the shackles and let her walk again? Her eyes sparkled with hope for a second, then returned to their normal self when Will let out a laugh. "Or I can keep you here like a filthy animal that you are. What do you think, Loretta?"

She put her head down while keeping silent.

"As always, you've got nothing to say."

He walked out of the room and came back, holding something large in his hands. "Get up," he ordered.

With difficulty, she stood up and fell to the floor immediately as her muscles gave up under her. The shackles around her ankle made it a lot harder for her to move, but she finally stood up, holding herself against the edge of the bed. On the other side, Will stood, waiting for her to rise.

"Lie down," he said.

On the bed, there was a fresh set of sheets, two pillows, and a blanket. She rolled onto the bed and placed her head on a pillow, shivering with fear and exhaustion. Will lied down next to her as if they were hanging in their mutual home bedroom, after a long day of working around the farm, and now it was time to sleep.

He drew the blanket and covered Loretta, rubbing her arm quickly. "You're shivering."

She nodded, but the nod went without notice.

They lay in bed like that for a few minutes. Loretta had nothing to say, though she had many questions. Suddenly, Will slipped his left arm from under her and hugged her around the neck. Her skin turned into goosebumps, fear shivering down her spine. She was certain he was about to harm her, reach out with another hand and strangle her. She squinted her eyes, awaiting her fate, wondering if she'd find her parents as soon as she crossed into their world. There was no time to cry, to mourn the fate, so she let out a sigh of acceptance.

She was ready.

To her surprise, Will kept his arm steady under her neck, occasionally turning his head to look at her.

He leaned forward and whispered in her ear. "Gosh, I've missed you, Loretta."

Then he let out a quiet sob.

CHAPTER 41

WILL SOBBED FOR A WHILE.

Loretta remained unmoved, afraid of either comforting or scolding him. He wiped tears off his face one more time and sniffled. "I fucked up, Loretta."

Loretta nodded. Killing Amy White? She was shocked at first that he'd willingly told her about the murder. But what did he care? Who was Loretta going to tell? She knew she wasn't coming out of this mess alive, especially now that she knew he'd killed Amy. The police, other than Will, still had to believe Loretta was involved in Amy's murder.

As if he read her mind, he said, "Can you fucking believe it? Amy was so feisty. As soon as I approached her, she recognized me." He shook his head. "When I grabbed her, she fought and pulled a pepper spray on me. I had to do something. I'm no longer sure it was the right thing to do, Loretta."

He glanced at her, squinting his eyes. His guilt oozed out of him.

Loretta inched toward the bed's edge, away from Will. He was a coward. Amy had to have been so frightened, and she acted accordingly. But his mistake shouldn't have warranted the death of an innocent woman.

Loretta wanted to scream out of angst, but she would be dead right on the spot. No one on earth could hear her, anyway, from the depth of those woods.

"Hey, Loretta, do you remember when we first met?" Will giggled like a high schooler.

"When we first started dating. Oh my God, that was the best fucking time."

Paying no attention to Loretta, he gazed into the distance, as if having a conversation with himself.

"Remember when we went into the woods and almost got lost?" He giggled. "Yeah. You grabbed my arm, because you were so scared, and your palms were so sweaty. But, you know, I loved how scared you were. You know why?"

Silence. Loretta listened intently, letting Will get it out of his system.

"You know why, Loretta? I was proving to be your man. I was there to protect you. I ... I loved how I found our way out, and when we got to the safe place, I remember you gave me a big-ass hug and kissed me on my cheek."

He sounded incredibly excited, as though he was about to burst into tears.

"Oh. And remember the prom? Oh. You looked like ...

I don't even know if I can describe what you looked like when I saw you walking down the stairs. I guess an angel is an understatement."

He looked at her for a split second, unable to discern her features, and continued. "Do you understand how it feels to be in love, Loretta? Like, when you love someone to pieces and all you do is think about them, daydream about your future with them. You want to get inside them and explore every inch of their being. Be part of them."

Will scoffed. "That's what I felt for you."

He swallowed to stifle a cry. "Look where we're now." He paused. "I killed Amy."

Loretta flinched and inched away. With a sudden movement, he turned his head towards her and firmly caught hold of her arm to make sure she didn't get too far away.

"I set you up," he said after a long silence.

Loretta's forehead creased, and her body stiffened. She had been set up, that was clear now. Though she still wasn't sure why he'd kidnapped her, and what his exact plan was.

"I was the one who put the bloody knife in the bakery." He paused again. "It was almost too easy."

He said it all in a voice of resignation. It made Loretta flinch once again. Amy White had been murdered with a knife she'd never laid eyes on.

"I knew they'd suspect you first. I've come up with a great motive for you." He laughed, then removed his arm from under Loretta's neck. "The whole town knows you're crazy. Of course, nobody was going to believe what you had to say. And everyone was going to believe me, a cop."

He laughed maniacally, then stifled his laughter with a single snort.

"And that whole story about your pregnancy and how you faked it. I mean, that topped it."

Under the moonshine, Loretta could see his face turn into an angry grimace. His jaws tightened, and his eyes glistened in the dark. He didn't look human at all.

She recalled the time they were together, and he made her wear a fake pregnancy belly, because he thought it would be a good omen. It would bring them luck. Maybe the second time around they'd be better off, bring a small human into the world. Then Loretta would be his forever, and they'd live a happy life.

"But no one knows the truth, Loretta. No one knows what you've done back in the day."

He stood from the bed and paced back and forth in front of the bed. The space was so small, there wasn't a lot of movement allowed in the confines. He persistently walked, as if he was thinking, coming with yet another plan, or simply coping with his thoughts.

He halted and turned toward her, and screamed at the top of his lungs, "God damn it, Loretta, why did you kill our baby?"

LORETTA AND WILL had become a popular item in high school.

Everyone was jealous. All the girls were jealous of Loretta, and all the boys of Will. They embodied a perfect couple, like a couple of movie stars from the TV or People's magazine. Physically, they matched each other, and no one could come close.

But emotionally, it was a different story. The relationship was fine at first. They laughed all the time, spent all their time together, attended high-school parties. Will was in a high school football league, and Loretta would attend every game and cheer him on. Sometimes, she'd bring friends, but as jealousy mounted, her so-called female friends ostracized her and stopped spending time with her. Eventually, Loretta ended up spending time only with Will.

Her friend Sarah lived a couple of houses away, but she was three years older than Loretta, and at their age, that difference seemed to be huge. Sarah and her parents, on rare occasions, would stop by the house to buy fresh eggs for Easter. Sarah and Loretta would sit on the front porch, and Sarah would tell Loretta stories, sometimes based on true events, and most of the time, made-up. Loretta believed both. She couldn't differentiate between real and fake.

That was when she started to behave strangely. She was a teenager, and her world seemed upside down and lonely. Will sent her letters to express his love for her, but she'd hide and tuck them in her drawer, hoping her dad wouldn't find them.

Because, at age seventeen, she was too young to date and have sex. If her dad had found out, he would have been devastated.

Two days after Loretta's seventeenth birthday, she found out she was pregnant. It would ordinarily be considered a gift, a new life to cherish, but Loretta wasn't ready to be a mother. For one, her mental state had declined. She was having delusions and living in her own world. Sometimes, out of nowhere, she'd snap and have a tantrum. Her father was a witness to too many things in the house being broken.

Something was wrong with Loretta.

Her father took her for a psychiatric evaluation where the doctors determined she had bipolar. A chemical imbalance of the brain. Something one could not control, but drugs could help with her ever-changing moods.

When she found out she was pregnant, she had no one

to confide in. The most natural person would be a mother, but she barely even remembered her. She had to tell her father, even though she knew he might disown her.

"Don't tell anyone, Loretta," he'd told her. "I want you to keep it a secret."

They were sitting at the dining table, her father looking disheveled, worried-sick about his young daughter.

Loretta had nodded, feeling ashamed.

"And I don't want you to hang out with that boy anymore. Do you hear me? He doesn't care about you. He only cares about himself."

Loretta gazed up at his father, not fully understanding what he had meant by it, but she nodded and placed her head back down.

She didn't listen to him, of course. A week later, she was lying in Will's bed, their hands interlaced. His mother worked two jobs to support her and Will, so she was almost never home. He was smitten by her, constantly daydreaming about their life together with a child. Loretta would wince at his words, and her heart would race out of her chest, afraid of crushing his dreams.

As they lay on the bed, he placed his hand on her belly. "I can't wait to meet the little one."

He placed his ear on the stomach, as if listening to the growing life. There was so much beauty and innocence in his gesture. Loretta wanted to cry, but if she tried to explain that she wasn't ready to be a mother, he would never understand. Not in a million years, because he'd already set his mind that he wanted to be a father.

She never told him her father took her to a hospital and made her have an abortion. He chose a hospital in Boston in the fear they'd run into someone they knew in the Athol hospital. Reputation was a big deal back in the day, and her father didn't want to compromise his, especially since he worked in a bank and relied on customer service for business.

But the town was small, and Will found out, anyway.

Loretta didn't think he would be upset too much about it. After all, he, too, was young, and had many life prospects to pursue. If he had a child, all his dreams would go down the drain, and then what? Eventually, he'd blame his terrible life and call it a prison with a wife with saggy boobs and a half-wanted child.

She had walked into his house, sensing something was wrong. Will seemed different. He didn't give her a kiss at the door like he usually did, and he seemed too quiet.

He took her hand and walked her to his bedroom. When they got there, he pushed her on it hard and handcuffed her to the bedposts. His expression shifted from intense focus to anger, and he purposely avoided making eye contact with her.

"What are you doing?" she'd whimpered. The handcuffs tightened their grip around her wrists, and an excruciating pain traveled through her body. If she screamed, it would be pointless. Instead, she bit down on her lower lip and hoped for the best. Hoped Will would cool down soon and let her go. For God's sakes, it wasn't like they were married or anything like that. They were only seventeen. He couldn't have been so enraged about it all.

He climbed on top of her, his eyes staring down at her. "I love you, Loretta, but you're a devil," he hissed. "You're a child murderer."

He slapped her hard across her face, making Loretta's ears ring. Tears welled up in her eyes, but she didn't make a sound. She should have listened to her father.

He stripped her naked and produced a knife out of thin air.

"What are you doing?" Loretta shrieked through her tears.

He glanced at her, then set the gaze upon her abdomen, tilting his head, studying her body. "I'm going to engrave my name on you, Loretta." He looked at her with an evil eye. "Even if you get away, you'll remember me forever."

He positioned the knife in his hand, brought his head closer to her body, then began to cut her.

CHAPTER 43

LORETTA WATCHED Will pace back and forth, his hands clenching and unclenching, his nostrils flaring.

It was obvious he had never forgiven her for what she did fifteen years ago.

Here they were again, playing out the same scene fifteen years later. Cutting her belly remained a secret, because she was too ashamed to admit what had transpired. And she certainly couldn't say anything to her father, as she had promised never to see Will again.

Loretta was in shackles, while Will, full of rage, controlled the whole situation. Or at least tried to. Who knew history would repeat itself?

But she knew she wasn't coming out alive this time.

Will stopped by the window and looked up at the moon. He put his hands on the windowsill and took a deep breath, as if sending calm through his body. He turned around and walked to the bed, plopping himself hard next to Loretta.

"Are you sleepy?" he asked.

Not sleepy. Exhausted. Lifeless and ready for all this to end. Not that Will would empathize or understand.

"Yes."

Maybe he would leave her alone. Maybe his rage would subside.

"Put your head on the pillow," he said.

Loretta inched toward the pillow, careful not to pull on the shackles too hard. The metal against her skin had been rough, causing the skin to peel and bleed. But like everything else, she was becoming numb to the pain.

When her head landed on the pillow, Will reached down and gave her a gentle kiss on her cheek. He wiped his mouth with the back of his hand and said, "Do you remember the last time we lay in bed like this?"

It was only three years ago Will had asked Loretta out when they ran into each other. Ever since her father had passed away, she'd been feeling lonely living in the house. Dating didn't pan out to be the most successful venture, so she thought she would give her high school fling another go. In her mind, she had thought Will had changed by then. He had to have softened over the years and become a responsible adult. After all, he was in law enforcement—they'd have to vet his personality, ensure he was sane enough to serve and protect the public.

The last time they lay in bed together was in fact in the mental facility. He came to visit her, lay next to her. She'd stared at the wall ahead and whispered, "Will, this is the end. I'm breaking up with you."

Her facial expression had remained stone-cold. As he got up and walked through the door, she bade him farewell in her mind, relieved this was over.

Before he headed out, he'd looked at her one more time and said, "Gosh, Loretta, why are you so... crazy?" He laughed at his quip.

Back in the cabin, he gave her a loose hug and ordered her to sleep. "Tomorrow is a long day. Let's get some rest."

She didn't expect him to stay overnight. She didn't feel any more at ease with him around.

He drew the blanket to his face and fell asleep shortly after. Loretta stared through the window as the moon moved behind the cloud, hiding and covering the vile shadows that had haunted her life.

CHAPTER 44

BY THE TIME Loretta woke up, Will was gone.

She felt the absence of his warm body as the cool air breezed through the room. Outside, it was raining cats and dogs, signaling that Fall was approaching. She lifted her head to examine the room but had a hard time keeping it up. The lack of nourishment made her weaker by the day.

He had left her in the same condition as before: shackled and locked up in the small room. She reflected on their conversation from last night. The mention of the baby was a surprise. By now, she had thought he would be over it, but who knew, maybe he was just looking for an excuse to act like a menace.

Loretta, to this day, tried to imagine what it would be like to have a child. An extra plate accompanied every meal she had served at home. What would it feel like to feed the child? To cook for one more person. To wash that one more dish. Perhaps she wasn't destined to be a mother, and that was okay. Some women weren't born to reproduce. When you lose your mother so early in life and don't have a concept of what motherhood entails, what were her chances of success as one?

The rainfall had ceased. The smell of the rain and the dew on the forest reminded her of growing up on the farm. The woods nearby. The forest was her sanctuary: it was a place she used to hide and spend time alone.

Loretta daydreamed and reminisced about old days. That was all she could muster during her captivity.

But maybe it was time to plot her escape, though she didn't know where to begin. The shackles on the wall were well secured and remained in place. She wasn't strong enough to yank it out of the wall. Shoot, she could barely lift her head on a good day. The thought of being captive indefinitely, then dying a terrible death, terrified her. She still had it in her to live a long life, care for her animals, find peace within. Maybe the plan would come to her eventually when she hit the rock bottom.

Survival mode has the power to drive remarkable accomplishments.

She heard steps outside the door and curled up in bed immediately. Will was mumbling something under his breath while he worked the lock on the other side of the door. He wore his police uniform this time, and as usual, he had a bag of food in his hand.

"Rise and shine." He mocked her. "You're getting a bath today."

Loretta creased her eyebrows, wondering if this meant he'd free her, at least temporarily, to complete the task. He threw the bag in her direction and said, "Eat first. I stopped by the bakery. Liz says hi." He laughed at his quip. Of course, Liz wouldn't send greetings to Loretta, even if she knew she was still among the living.

Loretta pulled the pastry out of the bag and ate it with zest. It was her favorite. Spinach rolls with puff pastry. Soon, she'd be fed and clean. Captivity had dehumanized her, and the food and cleanliness would bring some normalcy.

As she ate, Will kneeled and freed her ankle from the shackles. The riveting sound of metal dropping to the floor made her swallow.

"Stand up."

She was already done eating. She tried to stand up, but her legs were weak. Being anchored to the same spot and not using her muscles for days had done her in.

"I...I can't," she whispered.

"Jeez, Loretta." Will walked around and scooped up her tiny body. "Hug me."

She complied, even though she felt this was too familiar, too intimate. Too confusing since she knew this was a means to get her ready for her fate. He carried her like a child.

Now that they were outside the cabin room, she glanced around, finding herself in a tiny house that was made of brick. There was an old fireplace in a corner that no longer functioned, and in the other corner was a kitchenette with busted cabinet doors. The window above the kitchen sink had a big hole letting in some cool air from the outside. The cabin was uninhabitable. It looked like nobody had maintained it over the years.

Will seemed to have found its purpose.

They walked through the door into the outside, where trees and overgrown bushes surrounded them. Loretta gasped at the scenery, hardly believing she was witnessing the planet's beauty again. Her eyes welled up with tears and she closed them, because the outside light was too much to bear. She felt the bumpy movement of Will's body as he carried her to the back of the house, and gently placed her inside a bathtub. She peeled her eyes open and looked at the background of the beautiful forest and the tall trees swaying against the gray sky. The scenery looked like an unfinished painting; no colors added yet. She looked at him, wondering what was coming next.

"Take off your clothes," he ordered. He put his hand on the pistol hanging by his side and continued. "And don't do anything stupid. I'll be right back."

Don't do anything stupid. Even if she tried, she couldn't. She leaned against the cold tub, shivering, but she couldn't move much as her muscles ached.

When she mustered some strength, Loretta slowly peeled her camisole off, which was covered in blood, sweat, and dirt. Her underwear was disgusting, but worse things had happened.

Will returned with a large bucket of water in one hand and a soap bar in the other. He gave her a small smile when he noticed her naked.

He kneeled to the ground to face her at the same level, then stared at her for a few seconds. "Are you ready?"

She nodded shyly while covering her chest with her bare hands. Inside the bucket was a small scoop, and Will filled it with water before he poured it onto Loretta's head. The water was freezing, sending shivers down Loretta's spine. The air temperature was in the mid-seventies, but the earlier rain and tree shadows made the air colder. She shook, yet she was grateful for this experience. Her teeth chattered, and her skin turned to goosebumps.

Will kept pouring water onto her body until she was wet enough to add soap and he lathered it all over her. As he gently massaged her arms, lifting them, then rubbing her armpits, he'd glance at her occasionally and smile. "You know, I'm still your number one fan."

Loretta recalled his signature in the letters he used to send when they were in high school. It made her smile back then, but now she hated the sound of it. It sounded creepy. Out of place.

If he was her number one fan, shouldn't he treat her better?

He rinsed off the soap and reached for a worn towel. He covered Loretta and told her to stand up. The bath had invigorated her, so her movement became livelier. She stood up, and Will scooped her up again, carrying her back to her room.

She smelled the soap on her body, and she smiled inside. But as soon as he placed her on the bed, the fleeting happiness dissipated. The stench of her piss and feces brought her back to reality.

Will reached out for the chain to put the shackle back on her ankle. Loretta's eyes widened in fear, and she drew her legs closer to her face. When Will attempted to grab them, she started to kick and scream. "No, no, no! Please, please don't!"

Will was a lot stronger than her, so he took her ankle with ease and put the shackle back on. He was pissed. "I treat you so well, give you a bath, bring you food, and look what you've done."

He rubbed his hand that Loretta hit with her leg. "You feisty little thing."

He couldn't seem to look at her. "If you ever try to resist me again, I'm going to kill you," he said through his clenched teeth.

But Loretta knew this was his plan all along. Now she just needed to think of her escape.

CHAPTER 45

SMALL PLANS for her escape percolated in Loretta's mind, but nothing concrete and certain.

She stared down at the shackles, feeling helpless. Unless she could figure out a way to free herself from it, she was a prisoner forever, and there was no escape. But if she could get out of the shackles, the window was low enough that she could just open it and jump out and walk to her rescue. But the metal around her ankle would be hard to break unless she had a pair of pliers.

Her weak body gave in as she fell asleep mid-thought. Captivity exhausted her mentally, and while hope was the only thing that held her together, fear was most prominent.

She saw no end in sight.

Will's voice woke her up. He was back. Outside, it was already dark, but tonight, the moon was covered behind the clouds, preparing for imminent rain. Will was out of his uniform, wearing the same pair of jeans and a Celtics T-shirt. Loretta remembered he was a huge basketball fan and enjoyed driving into Boston to watch them live at TD Garden. Those things, like making a trip to Boston or attending a basketball game, seemed so foreign to her now. Almost like a fairy tale.

He hovered above the bed and watched Loretta with the flashlight of his phone projecting on her. He scrutinized her body as his eyes danced up and down. A flicker of lust sparked in his eyes.

"Take your clothes off."

She did as he asked. He stripped his jeans and boxers off and laid himself on top of her. Loretta smelled his familiar cologne, and it made her gag. He slid down and kissed her body, temporarily stopping to touch her scar. He dabbed it gently with his fingers and smiled. "Look, it's still here," he said, as if he was proud of scarring her for life.

He reached her crotch and kissed inside her thighs.

After propping himself up, he brought his hard penis to her face.

"Do it."

Loretta knew what he meant by it. Hesitant, she closed her eyes to lessen the impact of her shame, and cupped his penis with her mouth, feeling his skin. Tears streamed down her face, as she thought of the prisoner he had made her. This kind of humiliation was intolerable.

A wave of anger washed over her. As he slowly moved and throbbed his penis in her mouth, she bit him as hard as she could and held the bite for as long as she could.

Will's deafening scream made her ears ring. She let go, and Will reached for his crotch, feeling an enormous pain.

He yelled a string of profanities at her. As soon as the pain subsided, he charged Loretta with fists—he hit her with them everywhere: her face, her chest, her arms.

Will stopped when Loretta gave no sign of life or showed any movement. She lay in bed, lifeless, blood oozing from her nose and lips. He didn't bother to check if she was still breathing.

Ashamed, he stood from the bed. "That will teach you a lesson, you Goddamn whore."

CHAPTER 46

A WHOLE DAY could have transpired by the time Loretta woke up.

The ache in her body made itself known as she attempted to roll over and find a comfortable position. The new sheet was covered in blood, and it looked dried out and brown. She felt blood on her face and bumps above her eyes. She flinched and shrieked in pain as she dabbed her face. Will had been angry with her before, but not like this.

Loretta wondered if Will would come back, and what would happen if he did, but a gut feeling told her he might not. As she stared at the ceiling, one-eyed, she plotted her escape. For that to happen, she had to regain her strength and muster all the will inside her.

Under the bed, the uneaten can of sardines and an old bread were still there. She rolled herself over until she dropped to the floor, and the metal sound of shackles echoed in the room. She looked out the window and saw the tree branches swaying against the wind. Her mind conjured freedom, and she longed for it so badly that the survivor instinct began to kick in. She had to get out of here, and she would find a way.

She reached for the loaf of bread and dabbed it. It had turned stale and hard, but she didn't care. She nibbled at it slowly, cradling it in one hand and a dented can of sardines in the other, her stomach growling in protest. The meager rations, a pitiful sustenance that barely staved off hunger, were all Will had given her.

With a resigned sigh, she tore off a piece of the bread, and the dry crumbs fell onto the floor. She chewed slowly, the tasteless morsel sticking to the roof of her mouth. Each swallow felt like a chore, but she knew she needed to eat to maintain her strength, however feeble.

After finishing half of the loaf, Loretta turned her attention to the can of sardines. She struggled to pry it open with her trembling fingers, finally succeeding with a sharp twist of the lid. The pungent aroma of fish filled the air, making her stomach churn.

Using her fingers as makeshift utensils, she scooped out a few oily fish and placed them on a small piece of bread. Despite their strong flavor and slightly off-putting texture, she forced herself to eat them, knowing it was her only option for sustenance.

As she chewed, Loretta's mind drifted to thoughts of escape, her determination flickering like the lantern's flame. She couldn't remain captive in this forsaken cabin forever. But for now, all she could do was eat her meager meal and bide her time, hoping for an opportunity to break free from her captor's grasp.

Then an idea crossed her mind. Her one good eye widened. She finally had it.

But first, she had to finish her meal and get all the strength she needed to proceed.

CHAPTER 47

WILL HAD a hard time sleeping the night Loretta bit his penis hard.

He knew she was crazy, but never in a million years did he think she would bring herself to do something like that.

As soon as he opened his eyes in the morning, he felt anger all over again. He should have killed her right there and then, and maybe he did, given all the beating, but he would let someone else find that out. Even if he didn't kill her, she would, without a doubt, die there without food or water for days. She couldn't move with the shackles on, so death was imminent.

It was a good plan.

He checked himself and noticed the swelling on his crotch. He should probably pay a visit to the emergency room and check if her dirty mouth had caused an infection, but he was too embarrassed. Besides, what would he say to the nurse?

He didn't want any suspicions cast on him. In the meantime, he hoped the bite wouldn't cause permanent damage to the nerve. That could render him useless and impotent forever.

Giving her a death sentence gave him a pang of relief, and, in his mind, he had already said his goodbyes. No more Loretta.

At the police station, he kept to himself, sitting in his office, counting hours and days. He wasn't sure if the chief would be replaced or whether they would consider his candidacy, but he would apply when the time came. Now that he had used up all his tricks, the case of Amy White's murder wasn't going anywhere. There weren't any new leads, which didn't surprise him.

Detective Bradley walked into his office, standing at the door with his arms swinging by his side.

"Hey, Russell."

Will averted his gaze from the computer and looked at Detective Bradley. "Hey."

"You're looking rough. Everything okay?"

Bradley was referring to the bags around Officer Russell's eyes and his pale face stemming from a sleepless night. If Bradley only knew what had brought the rough look about, he would be in big trouble.

There was no reason for anyone to suspect him. Loretta remained the prime culprit. He'd played all his cards well, and now that the chief was gone, maybe he was still up for a promotion.

"Yeah, I just..." he paused... "I had a date last night."

"Oooo." Bradley's face brightened up. "Anyone special?"

Will nodded. "Very special." He gave him a small smile.

"Hey, you wanna grab lunch?" He pointed his thumb behind his back.

Will thought about it for a second. Socializing was the last thing on his mind, but he probably shouldn't say no. Maybe he could talk to Bradley about his career move, see what he thought of his possibility of being promoted. He stood up and proceeded to the door. "Oh, what the heck."

Bradley smiled. "Any good places around here?"

"Yeah. I've got a place," Will said. "We can just walk."

They walked through the police station and into the cool day outside. It had rained the day before, lowering the air temperature.

They arrived at the bar where Will used to have lunch all the time until recently. Andrea, the bartender, greeted him and told him to sit wherever they wanted. A couple were sitting at the bar, but it was otherwise empty.

When they sat down, Bradley took the menu and darted his eyes over it. "What's good here?"

"I usually have a burger or a Rueben sandwich."

Bradley closed the menu. "That sounds good."

They ordered and waited for food to arrive, having a small talk in between. When they finished their meals, Bradley leaned forward and placed his hands on the table, interlacing his fingers. He scrutinized Will's face until he broke the news.

"There have been some recent developments on the Amy White case, and I've been meaning to tell you. We've listened to the anonymous call about witnessing Loretta on the murder scene, and we're led to believe that the call was a hoax."

Will widened his eyes at Bradley and scoffed, "What? A hoax?"

Bradley nodded once. "That's right. We listened to the recording multiple times. The voice didn't seem natural. Something was off."

Will stared at Bradley and listened to him intently. He didn't like the way he spoke *at him*. Something about his tone seemed accusatory and wrong. Like he was blaming Will for the call. Like he was onto something that would just snowball and bring him to Will as the murderer.

He swallowed hard and waited for more.

"We also believe that the voice was masked. Whoever called, that wasn't their authentic voice. It was too high-pitched."

Will stared at him, speechless. He blinked a few times, abating the anxiety he was feeling in his chest. He pictured Amy's lifeless body lying on the ground after he'd stabbed her several times, then cut off her breast. Then the image of Loretta in the small room, with the shackles around her ankle, flashed in front of his eyes.

Gosh—he'd made so many mistakes. This whole thing took a terrible turn, and he didn't know how to react or what to say. But he should say something. He had to, in order to stay on course.

"Why would anyone want to fake a call?" he finally mustered.

Bradley kept staring at him. "The only reason I can think of is to divert from the actual killer."

The waitress came by and dropped the bill on the table. Will was relieved the tension had lifted even for a second.

As soon as she walked away, Bradley continued. "We also believe that Loretta has been framed. But why, we don't know. We can only speculate that someone is taking revenge against Loretta. Someone who knows her really well. Someone who has intimate knowledge about her past."

Will swallowed a lump in his throat, doing his best to conceal his anxiety.

"And, off the record, if I'm to venture a guess, Russell, I think you know a lot more than you've led us to believe."

CHAPTER 48

LORETTA'S HEART pounded in her chest as she surveyed the rusted shackles clasped tightly around her ankle.

They were a constant reminder of her captivity, digging into her skin with every movement. But today, she resolved, would be different.

Today, she would escape.

The cabin lay silent around her. She listened out for the sound of Will arriving, but her captor was likely occupied elsewhere. With trembling fingers, she stood up and approached the bed leg. In her mind, the only way to remove the shackles was if she broke her ankle so, broken and flexible, it could easily slide out of the shackle ring. All her life, she had never broken a bone, but there was time for everything. Desperate circumstances called for desperate measures, and she'd rather end up with a broken ankle than dead.

She was certain her plan would be successful if she were persistent. In the back of her mind, she prayed Will wouldn't show up. Because if he did, she could throw her escape plan down the drain. If Will found out what she was plotting, he would kill her on the spot. No questions asked.

Taking a deep breath to steady her nerves, Loretta positioned her ankle to the floor to allow for the bed to land on it. With all the strength she could muster, she lifted the bed, and then dropped it, allowing it to come crashing down on her ankle.

She screeched in pain, feeling dizzy, but she was sure her ankle was still intact. She wobbled it to make sure she was right, then positioned it again against the floor for another attempt. She picked up the bed and crashed it against her ankle, and the sound of the snapping bone echoed through the cabin.

She fell to the ground in unsurmountable pain.

The ceiling above her spun around from the dizziness the pain caused. Her ankle was broken. There was no question about it. But now she had to remove it from the shackles and be free. Once she could gather her wits and proceed.

Minutes passed like hours as she painstakingly worked at sliding her ankle out, her heart racing with every movement. Her leg hung limply, the bone protruding through her skin. That bone was disfigured, looking like it didn't belong in her body. She drifted her ankle through the ring; the pain throbbing through the body, sending dizzy spells to her brain. Things people did to survive.

Finally, her ankle was freed from the shackle, and a surge of triumph rushed through her veins.

The pain was excruciating. White-hot agony coursed through her body. Tears pricked at the corners of her eyes as she fought to suppress a cry of pain. But through the haze, she felt a sense of relief wash over her.

With trembling hands, Loretta pushed herself to her feet, her injured ankle protesting with every movement. But she refused to let the pain stop her. With a determined limp, she made her way to the window, her heart pounding with anticipation.

With a final glance back at the cabin that had been her prison for so long, Loretta threw open the window and breathed in the fresh air of freedom. The woods stretched out before her, beckoning her with their promise of escape.

Summoning all her strength, Loretta threw herself out of the window and into the unknown, her injured ankle screaming at her. But she paid it no mind, her adrenaline-fueled determination driving her forward.

As she moved into the dense foliage of the forest, Loretta sobbed tears of relief. With her newfound freedom, she would stop at nothing to reclaim her life.

CHAPTER 49

WILL SAT FROZEN IN PLACE, a rush of anxiety coursing through him.

"What are you suggesting?" Will stared at him with menace in his eyes.

But Bradley didn't flinch.

"Russell..." Detective Bradley gave him a small smile. "I've been at this for longer than you think. You were practically crawling when I first entered law enforcement."

Whatever, Will thought.

"Here's the thing. This is a small town. Murders and people missing don't happen often or at all. And definitely not within days of each other."

Will smirked. Bradley had a point. The last time Athol had a murder case was twenty years ago. Missing persons? Never.

"You never disclosed the fact you knew Loretta personally, Russell. Why is that? Don't you think it could be relevant to our investigation?"

Will's gaze dropped, and his shoulders slumped. Instead of answering the questions, his eyes darted around as if seeking an exit.

"Bad things don't happen in a sequence like this, Russell. Murder and disappearance." Bradley looked pissed. "It's too much of a coincidence that Chief Blake was caught in a scandal shortly after, then the secretary quit... the anonymous call... I think, Russell, you're trying to hide something."

But he didn't know or suspect half of it.

He had heard Bradley was a shark and the best homicide detective in the region. If he wanted to survive this, he needed to play his cards right.

Will's mind raced, his heart pounding in his chest as he tried to plan a response. He couldn't let Detective Bradley see through his facade, couldn't let him suspect for a moment that Will was anything other than innocent.

"I'm not sure what you're suggesting, Detective."

Will's voice sounded calm despite a hurricane inside.

"I'm not suggesting anything, Will," Bradley said, his tone deceptively even. "I'm simply pointing out the facts. And the fact is, you were the last person to see Loretta."

Will clenched his jaw, his fists trembling with suppressed rage. He had to tread carefully, had to turn this situation to his advantage without incriminating himself further.

"I don't know what you're talking about," he said, his voice barely above a whisper.

Bradley raised an eyebrow, his expression skeptical.

"You released Loretta from the police station, Russell, and she went missing the same day. Strange coincidence, don't you think?"

Will's mind raced, searching for a way to deflect suspicion. He needed an alibi, someone who could vouch for his whereabouts on the night of Loretta's disappearance. But his mind came up empty, the panic rising like bile in his throat.

"I didn't do it," he said, his voice shaking with desperation. "You have to believe me."

But Bradley's eyes remained cold and unyielding, his gaze boring into Will's soul with unnerving intensity. "Believe you? Why should I believe a man who's been lying to me from the moment I was assigned the case?"

Will's breath caught in his throat, his mind spinning with fear and uncertainty. He had to think fast, had to find a way out of this nightmare before it swallowed him whole.

"I'm telling you the truth," he insisted, his voice cracking with emotion. "I didn't kidnap Loretta. I swear it."

But Bradley's expression didn't waver, his skepticism etched in the lines of his face like a mask of stone. "When we go back to the station, I am requesting your removal from the case immediately. Got that?"

With that, Bradley stood up and strode out of the room, leaving Will alone with his thoughts and the weight of his own guilt.

As Bradley walked out the door, Will's heart sank, the truth crashing down on him like a tidal wave. He had thought he could outsmart them, could manipulate the situation to his advantage. But now, faced with the harsh reality of his actions, he realized he had only dug himself deeper into the pit of his own making.

He had killed Amy, had taken her life in a moment of blind rage and desperation. He'd abducted Loretta, convinced that she could shoulder all the burdens. And now, as the walls closed in around him, he knew there was no escaping the consequences.

But even as he faced the prospect of spending the rest of his days behind bars, a small voice whispered in the back of his mind, a voice filled with regret and remorse.

"I'm sorry, Amy," he whispered. "I'm so sorry."

EVERY MOVEMENT PROMISED FREEDOM, but it was too painful to keep going.

Loretta's legs gave up. It was too difficult to move with the broken ankle. She lay on the damp forest ground and began to crawl. She questioned where in the woods she was, as the surroundings looked vaguely familiar. Feeling disoriented, she let her instinct guide her to the safe place. She randomly picked a direction that she hoped was correct and yielded safety.

The day had just begun to form; the morning dew drying beneath her breath. The forest floor was rough under her body as she dragged it along. With the immense pain in her ankle, she felt the need to pause and gathered her wits, remind herself why she was doing this in the first place.

She wasn't ready to die.

The crawl would be long and gruesome. Even if it took

her all day to get to the destination, she would continue on the path. Now was not the time to give up. How far did she go? She turned around and saw the cabin behind her, a tiny smudge in the distance. She hadn't moved far, but she was making progress.

As she crawled, her garments were torn apart, leaving her vulnerable without the small shield she once had. Her ripped camisole exposed her skin, revealing deep scratches from the fallen tree branches.

Loretta stopped for a second to get her bearings. She scanned the surroundings with nothing in sight but the trees. She yearned for home as the birds in the nearby trees sang.

Even after scrutinizing the space, everything looked the same. The thickets all around gave her a familiar look, yet she was not sure if she had chosen the right direction. She wanted to scream for help, but she had no voice. Besides, what if Will returned to the cabin to check on her? She didn't want to give away her location, and it was important to remain incognito. Quiet.

She rolled over onto her back to gaze at the sky. Several birds flew past, bringing a smile on her face. It had been a while since she touched the ground, saw a bird, breathed in fresh air. She had freedom, yes, but would she survive the condition she was in: hungry, battered, thirsty, broken?

Across the sky, there were a few white clouds of no shape, but Loretta saw all sorts of animals whispering secrets. She heard her mother's voice telling her to hang on, to keep going. She closed her eyes, feeling a single tear travel down her cheek. Once again, she gathered strength with the adrenaline coursing through her veins.

When she accepted of the long path ahead, she rolled back onto her stomach and crawled again.

CHAPTER 51

AS WILL WALKED BACK to the police station, he made a choice. He had to kill Loretta. That was his last option.

Unless she was already lying dead in the cabin.

If he killed her and hid her body, she would still technically be missing, with no traces of her. That was a lot better than someone finding her in the cabin. Or her escaping. The former would be such a fucking disaster, he could never forgive himself for that oversight.

He reflected on his conversation with Bradley in the restaurant, and things looked grim. When he arrived at the police station, he'd learned that Bradley had already taken the steps he'd promised. Will was no longer assigned to the Amy White's murder case. And if they found more dirt on him, he would most likely lose his badge. Forget his career. Dreams. He might as well think of his exit plan and consider other career choices. Because being a cop didn't quite pan out.

How the fuck did he get himself into this mess?

The only person he could blame was Loretta.

He was too cocky to think everything would go splendidly, but there were people, like Detective Bradley, smarter than him. But maybe he could still outsmart him by removing Loretta from the equation. He'd kill and dismember her, bury her somewhere deep in the woods, where not a soul would find her.

Loretta, that menace of a woman, deserved to die. She'd made him lose his mind, sacrifice a body, lose his career—lose everything. He was certain she was a witch.

Will trudged through the dense forest, his feet cutting through the grass. He approached the secluded cabin nestled deep within the woods; its weathered exterior barely visible through the thick canopy of trees. The crunch of twigs beneath his boots echoed in the eerie silence of the afternoon.

Will's heart raced as he approached the cabin door, his hand instinctively reaching for his holstered gun. He paused, listening for any sign of movement inside. Silence greeted him. With a deep breath, he pushed the door open. The hinges creaked in protest.

Inside, the shadows shrouded the cabin, with the only light filtering in through the grimy windows. Will swept his eyes across the room, scrutinizing the sparse furnishings —a rickety old bed and a bucket in the room's corner. The chain lay on the floor, loose and forgotten. Will's world came crashing down around him.

Loretta was gone.

CHAPTER 52

LORETTA WAS EXHAUSTED BEYOND WORDS, but the adrenaline and the will to survive kept her going.

She dug her fingers into the damp forest floor, inching toward the border. In a glimpse of hope, she was sure she heard car tracks against the road, zooming by, and she pictured herself landing where help could be obtained right away.

It was just her ears ringing.

Branches snagged at her clothes as she pushed her way through the undergrowth, the forest floor damp beneath her body. Each rustle of the leaves sent a shiver down her spine, her senses heightened to the slightest sound or movement.

After what felt like an eternity, Loretta finally emerged into a small clearing. She paused for a moment, her chest heaving with exertion, before steeling herself for the last leg of her journey. She couldn't afford to let her guard down now, not when freedom was so close within reach.

With renewed determination, Loretta set off once more, her eyes fixed on the distant glow of lights that beckoned. She crawled through the underbrush, her limbs aching with exhaustion, but she refused to give up.

A single tear escaped her eye. She wiped it away with trembling fingers.

A voice calling her name and travelling through the woods made her blood freeze.

"Loretta! Where are you? I know you're here somewhere."

At first, she thought she was imagining it. Exhaustion could easily lead to hallucinations. As she froze to listen in to the sounds, the voice reemerged. A little closer.

"Loretta! Show yourself! I won't harm you."

Will. She recognized that voice immediately. It was filled with rage. In her mind, there was no way he would not harm her. She was certain her survival was at peril.

If Loretta could only make herself disappear. Like with a magic wand. But that angry voice brought her back to reality. She was filled with a tangible fear as her impending death approached.

Either the voice seemed to get closer, or the hollow forest projected his voice loudly. The sound of leaves rustling was impossible to ignore, and it was drawing nearer and nearer. Hoping to go unnoticed, Loretta tried to hide, but in the open woods, she would be easily visible.

She stopped, barely breathing. She pictured Will finding her and taking his gun to shoot her in the back of her head. Her brain splattering all over the ground.

His voice was getting even closer, and he had to be less than five hundred feet away. Her heart pounded in her chest as she pictured his discovery.

"Loretta!" Now the voice was close, within the reach, and she dreaded what was to come.

Maybe she should capitulate and beg him for his forgiveness. His punishment didn't equal the crime. Maybe she could somehow put sense into him and make him see things differently. Maybe they could start all over again. God help her.

"Loretta." His voiced halted suddenly, as if he'd finally spotted something shocking. "Loretta, I see you."

More leaf rustling. Then the words, "What the..." came out of his mouth before a shot out of a pistol was heard. Then another one. And another one.

Loretta covered her head with her hands, sure she was dead.

She felt nothing.

But she could still hear birds chirping and leaves rustling from behind. Did death sound like birds?

Someone grabbed her, and she flinched, assuming it was Will. She closed her eyes, unsure what was happening. Did he not shoot her after all? Did he decide to torture her some more?

With a gentle touch, he turned her around, causing Loretta to question if he had forgiven her. He was careful not to hurt her, his arms avoiding places where bruises turned blue and purple.

"Loretta."

She was confused. It wasn't like she hadn't heard that voice before. When she opened her eyes, she found him gazing at her with a worried expression.

"Loretta, you're safe."

It was only after she observed him more carefully that she discovered the person holding her was Bob.

CHAPTER 53

"BOB," Loretta whispered.

She reached for his face to make sure he was real, as if to check that she wasn't dreaming.

"I've found you." He smiled.

"How did you know?"

Well, that was the thing. He didn't.

That Bob happened to be there was a miracle.

The night before, he and Liz had gotten into a big argument, like they had a lot lately. The bakery was getting in worse shape, and their customer base was dwindling. The opposite of what Bob expected. But the bakery wasn't the only problem in Liz and Bob's marriage. Even the smallest things seemed to be the point of contention. They'd bickered in the past, but lately, their fights turned belligerent and violent where Liz would throw wineglasses at Bob as soon as she had a little to drink.

Liz could sense that their marriage was falling apart, and she blamed everyone but herself. Including Loretta.

Bob secretly thought Loretta could be part of it, but he would never admit to his wife. He'd tell her she was going crazy and should consider therapy, which enraged Liz even more.

The night before, Liz went over the top. She not only got drunk and threw things at Bob, but she told him to get the fuck out of their house and never return.

Bob slept at their cabin that night. Its conditions weren't the best, but, hey, it beat the car! That was the only solution at the time to stay away from his enraged wife. She was angry at life, and there was nothing he could do to help her.

That afternoon, he'd taken a walk in the woods. Ordinarily, he didn't carry his gun, but that morning, he removed the plank on the floor and took the gun, hiding it in the inside pocket of his light jacket. If he ever returned home, when Liz calmed down, he'd take it with him, even though he wasn't planning on using it. But it could come in handy. He could threaten his life with it in front of Liz.

Maybe that would shut her up for good.

Or else he was ready to divorce her. Tell her to scramble. Life was too short to be with the woman he no longer admired and loved. He was certain the feeling was mutual.

During his walk, he heard the male voice calling for Loretta. He hastened his steps and ran toward the voice. The anger in the voice was palpable, and as he got closer, he seemed to have recognized it better.

It was Will, the town cop.

Bob didn't like the guy. Every time he stopped by the

bakery, he acted like he owned the town. Since Bob strived to be polite to all his customers and be in good standing with the town cops, he had to mask his dislike for him.

His voice kept calling for Loretta, and Bob knew she was in trouble. Not to mention that he never believed she had anything to do with Amy White's murder. No way. Loretta might be eccentric, but she was good-hearted and a decent human being. Some life troubles that were unleashed on her were beyond her control.

When Bob saw Will walking in the woods, he noticed a gun in his hand aimed at an unseen target. Will fired a shot in the air, aiming at Loretta. That was when Bob pulled the trigger. Once. Twice. First Will's heart, then his head. It was an instinctive reaction that shocked Bob. But he'd do everything for Loretta. No one could harm her. He saved her life.

Bob lifted Loretta, determined to get her to the hospital right away. She glanced at the ground where Will's body lay, lifeless.

Bob carried her through the woods, occasionally glancing at her with a smile. His car wasn't that far off. He'd put her in the back and drive her to the Athol hospital. She needed immediate care, as the road to recovery was long.

As they trudged through the woods, she'd gaze at him occasionally in disbelief. Finally, when she offered him a smile, he said, "You'll be fine, dear. I would never let anything happen to you."

CHAPTER 54

THE ATHOL HOSPITAL was on the same strip as Loretta's old high school and the state police department. Traffic was light, but Bob rushed and took shortcuts to get there as soon as possible.

As soon as they crossed the hospital front door, Bob yelled for help. The hospital staff responded immediately, placing Loretta on a stretcher. There was no time to ask what transpired; time was of the essence.

"Please. Please take care of her," Bob whispered as they wheeled her to the emergency room. He stood still, witnessing his beautiful Loretta being granted another chance at life.

Loretta was disheveled, her once vibrant features now marred by bruises and scratches, her clothing torn and stained with dirt. Every movement seemed to carry the weight of an unfathomable ordeal.

Her hair, once meticulously styled, hung in tangled strands around her face, partially obscuring her hollow eyes. Those eyes, usually bright with life, now held a haunting emptiness, a silent witness to the horrors she had endured. Dark circles underscored them, evidence of countless sleepless nights spent in terror.

Her cheeks, once flushed with health, were now pallid and streaked with tears, each tear leaving a trail through the grime that coated her skin. Her lips, usually curved in a gentle smile, were now split and swollen, a reminder of the violence she had endured.

As she made her way into the hospital, she clutched at her clothing, as if seeking solace in the tattered fabric. Her movements were slow and labored, as though she bore the weight of the world upon her shoulders. Every breath she took seemed to come with a struggle, as if the very act of breathing was a painful reminder of the captivity she had escaped.

Her arms, usually slender and graceful, were now marked with bruises and abrasions. Each mark told a story of suffering, of agony endured in silence, hidden away from the world.

The hospital staff admitted her immediately and put her in a room on the second floor. She was safe.

At last.

DETECTIVE BRADLEY LISTENED in shock as Bob confessed to killing a man. He'd come to the station of his own accord and gone willingly into the small room where Loretta had recently been questioned. The tables had turned and now Loretta was seen as a victim and no longer a fugitive. He couldn't wait to find out what had transpired.

Bob had no qualms about volunteering all the information he knew about the case. He told Detective Bradley what transpired, and that he ran across Officer Russell with a gun pointing in the air, calling for Loretta who was in proximity. If Bob hadn't come to her rescue, Will would have killed her, hands down.

Detective Bradley scratched his head, wondering how Russell got himself killed in the depth of the woods. The odds of that happening were awfully low, unless there was some dispute he was involved with. When he found out that Loretta had been found battered and barely alive, pieces started to fall together.

While Detective could understand the facts, there was one question he was missing the answer to: why?

Why did Officer Russell want to kill Loretta? And why did he kidnap her?

She was considered a fugitive and the prime suspect in the Amy White murder. That he kidnapped her made little sense.

That afternoon, Officer Russell's death was all over the news. Made national TV as well. The police were still investigating as they suspected it could be related to Amy White's murder, leaving it a mystery.

Detective Bradley was hoping for a break. And it came that very same day.

———

The police station was quiet when the front door opened. The cool breeze whooshed in, signaling a cold season coming.

It had been less than twenty-four hours since Loretta was found, and everyone in town knew about it and that Officer Russell was gone. Shock multiplied, as this would be a second murder in less than a month. First Amy White, then Officer Russell. Who was next?

But the visitor was about to shed new light on the case.

Marybelle walked into the police station gingerly, fear

written all over her face. She approached the front desk where her replacement stared at the computer, not noticing Marybelle standing there.

Marybelle cleared her throat, drawing attention to herself.

"May I help you?" the new secretary said.

"Yes." Marybelle's voice was shaking. "I'm looking for Detective Bradley."

The front desk woman scrutinized her.

She disappeared from around the corner, silent, then reemerged seconds later. "Follow me."

Marybelle looked around the familiar place she'd spent a couple of years working. She knew all about how the police station operated, where the confidential files were kept locked, what each of the officers wanted in their coffee. She couldn't say she didn't miss it, but the relief from quitting so she didn't have to deal with Will any longer was worth it.

Now that he was dead, she could come forward and talk.

"Wait here." She brought her to the conference room and went back to her desk.

A minute later, Detective Bradley walked in, looking somewhat surprised to see her. "Hey, I know you."

He greeted her with cheer in his voice while Marybelle grew more anxious, and she gripped her purse more tightly.

"Are you back for the job?" he quipped.

"No." She shook her head. "I'm here to tell you what Officer Russell did...when he was still alive."

Detective Bradley sat down, his level of interest rising. "Do tell."

She fell silent, gathering strength to speak up. She looked up at the detective and said, "The anonymous call... that was me. He made me call the police station and tell them I saw Loretta near the murder scene that night."

She put her head down in embarrassment while the detective stared at her, his face expressionless.

"And it wasn't true. I didn't see her. In fact, I was at home, sleeping when it happened." Tears sprung from her eyes.

Detective Bradley pushed a box of tissues sitting on the table and said, "That's okay. I appreciate you coming forward."

Marybelle blew her nose and wiped the tears from her face.

"He also told me that if I say anything about the fake call, he will kill me. I believed him. I was too scared to come forward."

Silence fell upon the room, giving him time to absorb the information.

"I'm sorry," she said.

Detective Bradley didn't seem surprised. He asked Marybelle to describe the circumstances under which he forced her to call.

"Did he say anything else?"

"Yes." She paused as she pondered how to best to say it.

"What did he say?" Bradley's voice was calm.

She gazed down at her hands, interlacing her fingers, and said, "That he was doing Loretta a huge favor."

CHAPTER 56

DETECTIVE BRADLEY WAS AT A LOSS.

He suspected Russell most likely had something to do with Amy White's murder, but the puzzle pieces were missing. He hoped that some of them could be found in Russell's apartment. Right away, he requested a search warrant and got it within a day.

Russell lived in an apartment on the top floor of a building overlooking the Athol downtown. The views of the long main street and spare cars were underwhelming. Detective Bradley parked in the only available parking slot, which he assumed was for guests. They weren't labeled, and the building looked like a shithole, and it was obvious that the management didn't care for it well. But they were kind enough to respond to his request and unlock the front door of Will's apartment.

He cracked the door open and entered his home. It was a modest bachelor abode with an open concept of the living room, dining room, and the kitchen, with no dining table and chairs and a single couch and TV in the living room. The apartment smelled relatively clean, not like some shitty bachelor pads Detective Bradley had seen in his lifetime. For that, he was grateful as he walked around the space to study it.

He found nothing special about it.

On the kitchen counter, there were two framed photographs: one of young Will in a police uniform, smiling, and in the other, an older, sad looking woman. It had to be his mother, he decided, noticing the similar nose and droopy eyes in their facial features. He had heard that Will's mother suffered from dementia and had lived in an assisted living home, but Will never mentioned her to him.

There are those who opt out of conversations regarding matters that don't consume their thoughts or hold importance. Regarding his mother, Bradley wondered which it was for Will.

Someone needed to break the news to his mother that her son had died. She might or might not remember him. And for any mother losing a child, it might be better if she didn't.

On the counter was also a big case of protein shake powder, chocolate flavored. Bradley smiled, because that was the exact one he'd made for himself every morning. At least Russell had good taste. It was good stuff.

Bradley opened the kitchen cabinet drawers, looking for clues about his life. It was obvious he had harmed Loretta, but the murder case of Amy White was still open, and no leads had been found. Bradley imagined it could all be related, but he didn't have a slightest idea how or why.

As he rummaged through the kitchen drawers, a single knife drew his attention. It was tucked in the back of the drawer. The detective took it in his hand and turned it around and around until a spark of a clue flickered in his mind.

The brand name written on the knife was the same as the one found in the bakery.

Bradley almost gagged at the realization and nearly dropped the knife on the floor. He felt he had something here he could further investigate.

Not letting the knife out of his hand, he walked deeper into the apartment, stumbling upon three more doors. The middle one led to the bathroom, and Detective Bradley found nothing unusual about it. One, on the left, led to a room, which Bradley assumed was Will's primary bedroom. The smell inside was stale, the windows shut. The curtains were half-drawn, letting in some light to a dark place. In the center of the room was a king-size bed, its sheets and covers all wrinkled and undone. Two tables on each side were adorned with a lamp and some old photos of Will, half-naked. Bradley took one in his hand and stared, his eyebrows creasing. He had never seen someone place photos of themselves sitting next to their bed. Russell must have really loved himself. A dresser was on the opposite side, which proved to be empty.

No significant clues were present.

Bradley exited Will's bedroom and walked across the

hall to study the other room. As he cracked the door open, a deep silence and darkness greeted him. He could see nothing. The room resembled a dark room where Bradley used to develop films during his youth. He shook off the memories, attempting to stay in the present. A strange feeling rattled his nerves as he anxiously searched for the light switch on the wall.

Bradley entered the room when the lights turned on, and he was astonished by the sight before him.

"Holy cow," he whispered.

He could barely breathe. On each wall, there were giant pictures of Loretta:

Loretta smiling.

Loretta sad.

Loretta angry.

Loretta crying.

And next to each photo, there was an inscription written with a black marker:

Loretta, I love you

You'll always be mine

Don't be sad.

We got this!

As Bradley turned around to study the walls, one picture stood out from the rest. In it, Loretta was completely defaced with demon ears and scary eyes.

Loretta, I will kill you.

The letters looked like a three-year-old had written them. But the marker suggested it had to be done recently, perhaps a week ago.

Bradley dropped the knife, unable to breathe, feeling sick to his stomach. He was perturbed to think that Russell, supposedly a rising star in the law enforcement, was nothing but a psychopath.

He reached for his phone and dialed the police station.

"Hey, Dan. I need back-up. Send someone to Russell's place. We have got more evidence here."

CHAPTER 57

WHILE LYING in the hospital bed and staring helplessly at the ceiling, Loretta felt like all this was a dream.

A nightmare.

While her body was glued to the bed, her mind still wandered to the lonely cabin in the middle of the woods. When she closed her eyes, Will's face would appear; his stare looking menacing, his lips tight with rage. Part of her felt relieved that she was free from his clutches, and part of her felt terrified it could have been her losing life had it not been for Bob.

The sound of the door opening got her out of her thoughts. She gazed at the door and saw Sarah standing there, stunned. Her mouth was agape, and her eyes bulged at Loretta, examining the situation.

"Loretta," she said. "Oh, my God."

Sarah approached the bed, giving Loretta a small hug. She said that she'd never have assumed Loretta would be in this type of trouble, since, usually, Loretta *was* the trouble. It never occurred to her that someone might have set her up or that things could have gone terribly wrong. That, in fact, she wasn't "missing," but that someone might have kidnapped her.

She squeezed her hand. "I'm sorry for everything, my friend."

Loretta was happy to hear the word—friend—and smiled at Sarah.

"It's okay. None of us could have seen it coming, really."

"At first, I thought it was the guy I found at your house."

Loretta creased her eyebrows. "Ethan?"

Sarah shrugged. "I don't even know his name. I tried to ask him where you were, but he didn't want to speak with me. Strange fellow."

Loretta nodded. "He was."

"Who is he?"

Loretta shrugged. "A guy I was seeing. Didn't work out."

And what ever happened to Ethan? Loretta never heard from him again. Good riddance. He wasn't the guy for her. He would never fully understand her.

"I can't believe Will did this," Sarah finally said. "I knew him from the neighborhood. I thought he was a decent guy."

Loretta gazed at Sarah, struggling to accept the truth.

"Who knew people could be so cruel?" she said.

Loretta stared at a spot, her memories from the cabin flooding all over again. Everything went so wrong.

But they didn't have to. If they thought things through, Amy could still be alive, and Loretta could enjoy her peaceful life on the farm. But Will was hard to reason with. Not to mention their history—it was too complicated, and he never forgave her for it.

"Well, yeah," Loretta whispered.

"Do you mind if I write a book about this? A true crime novel?" Sarah asked sheepishly.

Loretta smirked. "I don't care."

"When the dust settles, maybe we can get together, and I can interview you. I'd love to know why you think he abducted you. This psycho." She chuckled nervously.

"Okay." Loretta nodded.

They sat in silence, Sarah looking at Loretta, biting down on her lip. "Speaking of which, did...did Will say anything to you that was out of place before he died?"

Loretta could see Sarah's mind churning with questions, already plotting her story.

For the first time since she was found in the woods, Loretta cast a wide smile across her face and said, "Yes, he did." She stared at Sarah and said, "He told me he killed Amy."

———

It took Loretta a couple of weeks to move and function.

Her body had deteriorated, but she would ultimately recover and hopefully go back to her old self. Her ankle had mostly healed, and she could walk albeit slowly. Two weeks after being at the hospital, she got discharged and sent home.

On a chilly day, she called an Uber to the police station at Detective Bradley's request.

They were sitting in the small interrogation room; the same one Russell and Blake took her to when the news about the murder broke out.

Detective Bradley set his eyes on her, not letting go of his stare. While more coherent in speech, Loretta knew she looked different from the last time he saw her. Broken and lifeless. But there was still a spark somewhere that just needed to be ignited and spread inside.

Time could heal, and she hoped it would.

He questioned her about her captivity in the cabin, and Loretta spoke softly, hesitantly, as if she was reliving the entire experience again. The memory of it all made her flinch. Detective Bradley scrutinized every word she spoke, as if weighing them between the truth and lies, but he nodded occasionally as if he could tell Loretta was telling the truth.

About thirty minutes in, he got the break he was hoping for. Loretta told him Will had admitted that he'd killed Amy. He questioned her repeatedly about that conversation to make sure it was the truth. Her speech was genuine. She couldn't lie. At this point, she had no reason to.

To confirm, she took a polygraph test, confirming the truth. Bradley looked relieved.

"Why do you think he killed Amy White?" he asked.

Loretta stared at him with wide eyes, looking thorough him, as if he was invisible, shaking her head and shrugging her shoulders. "I don't know."

EPILOGUE

One month later

SOMEONE KNOCKED on Loretta's door.

At a little after seven in the evening, the sun's rays stretched across the woods, casting shadows below. Loretta flinched at the knock, as she didn't expect any visitors. Who could it be at this time of day?

Nowadays, any slight movement around the house put her in a panic mode, thinking she was about to be kidnapped and taken again. The recent experience had a profound effect on her psyche, and she'd already sought therapy to confront the trauma. And a slew of other things.

The doorbell rang again, and she gingerly stood up from the couch. Before she approached the door, she stopped by the kitchen and grabbed a knife, just in case. She trudged to the door, then looked through the peephole. The image of the man standing on the porch took her by surprise. A flush of red spread across her cheeks and neck when she saw Bob standing, fidgeting around, looking away.

She hid the knife behind her back and opened the door.

When Bob saw her, he smiled, his arms hanging at his sides.

"Hi," Loretta said.

She played with the knife behind her back, touching and feeling the sharp blade only so lightly.

"Hi, Loretta."

"Hi," she said again, feeling awkward.

He scanned her up and down. "How are you feeling? Recovered yet?"

"Yeah, yeah, getting there. Thanks for asking." She offered a small smile.

"Well, you look good."

"Thanks," she said shyly. They stared at one another for nearly a minute until Loretta asked, "Can I help you?"

"Yeah," Bob said. "My car has broken down."

He gave a sideway look and laughed nervously. Loretta shook her head, "No, Bob. Please. No. Not today."

He lowered his head in shame and nodded quickly. "I get it. No problem."

She looked at him with empathetic eyes and considered letting him in, but she'd been in the middle of something important when he appeared at her door.

"You know, Liz and I are now separated."

Loretta squeezed the knife a little harder and pictured

stabbing Liz with it. That whore had always hated her for no reason at all.

"Oh, good." She assumed it was the right thing to say.

"Yes. It is," he said. "Listen, if you ever need anything, I'm here for you. Okay?"

Loretta smiled and nodded. "Thank you, Bob. You've already done plenty. You've saved my life."

She thought of ways to repay him, but no action could compare to saving a life. She knew what Bob ultimately wanted. He wanted her, but she didn't consider herself the best prize.

"Well, anything for you, Loretta," he said. "Oh, and by the way…if you want your job back at the bakery, you can have it. You know where to find me."

"Oh!" Loretta's voice pitched. "I may take you up on it."

Why not? She had no prospects, and getting any other job in this small town was often out of reach.

"I hope you do. Liz no longer takes part in day-to-day at the bakery. You won't have to deal with her."

Her grip on the knife loosened, as she felt relieved to hear that. "That sounds good, Bob." They paused and stared at each other for a second. "Well, thank you for your visit."

Loretta closed the door as she said goodbye. Bob mustered another smile and waved at her awkwardly. "Well. Okay. Bye."

Loretta checked out Bob through the peephole once again. He looked a lot healthier and invigorated than the last time she saw him, which was when she was first hospitalized. He looked around as if lost, then finally turned around and trudged to his car.

Bob was a good man, but he wasn't for her. She knew it in her heart.

She put the knife back in the kitchen and sat on the couch, getting back to her activity. She had found the box with the letters sitting on the basement floor, and she knew immediately Ethan must have read them when he was down there. Anger rushed through her, realizing he'd gotten into her personal space. But that was in the past. Ethan was history, and she had moved on from him.

She took an envelope sitting in a box and pulled the paper out of it. She recognized Will's familiar writing, but the last letter he wrote was a hot mess. His writing looked like a scribble written by a small child. And it was not surprising since they had just broken up and he was upset.

Her eyes darted to the page, tears welling her eyes, and she began to read:

Loretta,

My heart aches right now. After everything we've been through, I can't believe you broke up with me.

It's been months now, but I can't stop thinking of you, Loretta. You are the heart of my soul and a rose in my garden.

I thought I was completely healed from our breakup, but lately I realize I'm wrong. What we had was amazing. It was my sustenance. I haven't felt so close to another person before or since. Even when I think I'm over you, I constantly tell myself that I'm at peace with everything and that I'm over you—today I realized that if I were truly over you, I wouldn't have to constantly assure myself of it.

But you tell me things are over for good, and I don't believe you mean it. You just want to hurt me more and convince me we're not for each other. But I'm still not convinced.

You tell me, to prove my love for you, I should sacrifice a life. Loretta, you must be going crazy.

Even though I love you, I will never harm another human being to prove something. I don't know why you would even suggest I sacrifice a body to prove I love you. Everyone in town seems to think you're crazy, but I think you're just confused.

No one should die for love.

No matter what happens, I will always treasure the time we spent together. You have given me the most precious moments of my life. Maybe we will reunite someday. Maybe you will wake up one day and realize I was the best for you, and you for me. And until that day comes, I will live in hope.

Meanwhile, I will always be your number one fan.

. . .

THE END

I sincerely thank you for reading *Loretta*!

Did you like the book?

Please consider leaving a review, even if it's only a sentence, checking out my other books, or subscribing to my website: https://nadijamujagic.com

Did you love *Loretta*?

Fantastic! If you loved Loretta's journey, you'll definitely want to stay tuned for my upcoming releases. Join my Advanced Readers team by emailing me at nadijad@gmail.com

Would you like to read a deleted scene from *Loretta*?

Discover an exclusive deleted scene from the book that delves into the heart-wrenching conflict of Father Lee. In this scene, he grapples with the shocking news that Loretta, the troubled woman he has long tried to help, is the main suspect in a tragic murder case.

DOWNLOAD BELOW:

https://storyoriginapp.com/giveaways/5a3bd548-3c79-11ef-850f-bb0e5b1c95f9

ACKNOWLEDGMENTS

As an indie author, I don't get to work with the army of people it takes to produce a book. However, there are several people who have been instrumental in my writing journey whom I'd like to thank. Writing can be difficult and lonely, and sometimes, we writers need reassurance that our words are meaningful and not a waste of time. A trusting circle is important, and I am happy to know I have it.

Jessica Ryn, your editing skills are unparalleled. I am so grateful to you for making my books polished and shiny. I have full confidence in myself, and pushing the "publish" button when the time comes is easier because of you. Thank you for all your great comments and edits. You are brilliant!

Many thanks to the members of the Cops and Writers Facebook group, who patiently and quickly answered all my questions about police procedures. I am obviously ignorant when it comes to them, but I'm so glad I could rely on this amazing and knowledgeable group.

I appreciate my mother-in-law, Christine, who is so well-read, for being my alpha reader.

Thanks to Connal Orton for inadvertently being my

ARC reader and giving me some valuable insights into the manuscript. I hope we will collaborate someday!

Many thanks to Alison Osborn for catching and pointing out those pesky little typos and inconsistencies at the last minute. Your kindness is truly appreciated.

A million thanks to my husband, Chad Vecitis, who got me started with writing as my second career. I appreciate your support, encouragement, and objectiveness in this competitive and ever-changing vocation. You are my rock, and I love you to the moon and back.

To my little munchkin, who melts all my problems away in his presence, I am so grateful you exist in this world. You are the sunshine whose rays reach distant galaxies. You are the most inquisitive, fun-loving, and funniest three-year-old I've known, and I am so glad to call you my son. I love you so much it hurts.

Thank you, reader, for giving this book a chance and reading it to the end. I know books are read subjectively, but I hope it gave you some escape from the real world and entertained you.

SUBSCRIBE

If you'd like to keep up to date with my latest releases, or get news about occasional free or discounted books, please sign up at the link below. We'll never share your email address and you can unsubscribe anytime:

https://nadijamujagic.com

Nadija Mujagić was born and raised in Sarajevo, Bosnia and Herzegovina, what used to be the former Yugoslavia back in the late 1970s. In 1997, she moved to the United States shortly after the end of the Bosnian War and has lived in Massachusetts since. In her spare time, she enjoys playing sports and electric bass guitar. *Loretta* is her ninth book.

ALSO BY NADIJA MUJAGIC

Non Fiction

Ten Thousand Shells and Counting: A Memoir

Immigrated: A Memoir

Fiction

Till a Better World: Woman's Fiction

The Brilliant Mirage: A Thriller

The Exchange: A Psychological Thriller

The Master of Demise: A Psychological Thriller

The Nightmare Under the Mistletoe: A Christmas Thriller Novelette

Lottery Series (Gripping Psychological Thrillers) : 1) Lottery of Secrets

2) Lottery of Lies, 3) Lottery of Revenge

www.ingramcontent.com/pod-product-compliance
Lightning Source LLC
Chambersburg PA
CBHW061652190726
48289CB00006B/1843